A Dream of
Hunger Moss

A Dream of Hunger Moss

Mabel Esther Allan

DODD, MEAD & COMPANY

New York

Copyright © 1983 by Mabel Esther Allan
All rights reserved
No part of this book may be reproduced in any form
  without permission in writing from the publisher
Distributed in Canada by McClelland and Stewart Limited, Toronto
Manufactured in the United States of America
Illustration by Bertram M. Tormey

1 2 3 4 5 6 7 8 9 10

Library of Congress Cataloging in Publication Data

Allan, Mabel Esther.
  A dream of Hunger Moss.

  Summary: A girl visits Hunger Moss just before
World War II and seems to relive the experiences of
her mother who visited the same moor just before
World War I.
  [1. England—Fiction] I. Title.
PZ7.A4Dq 1983   [Fic]   83-14036
ISBN 0-396-08224-6

Contents

A Dream of
Hunger Moss

1 In Green Street

Hunger Moss haunted my early childhood; a dream place that I never expected to see in reality. I think it haunted Adam's, too, but to a lesser extent, because the stories stopped when I was about ten and Adam eight. After that Mother didn't talk much about her youthful adventures, maybe because we were too old to listen to stories mainly told at bedtime.

Reality was Green Street in Liverpool, and Dad's little store on Smithdown Road nearby, that took all his time but never made much money. And it was school, the high school, that I loved and where I worked so hard.

The summer I am writing about I was thirteen, going to be fourteen on September 3, and it was 1939.

My name is Alice Mary Baker. Alicia Marianne would be nicer, but Mother likes plain, old-fashioned names.

The street where we lived wasn't well named, either, because there was almost no green in sight. No trees, and hardly a blade of grass or a solitary weed pushing up among the old paving stones. Many of the streets around had country-sounding names, but the country was quite unknown to me then. The nearest I'd ever come to the country was a Liverpool park. If we had a

9

day out we usually took the ferry across the Mersey to Wallasey and played on the beach. Dad had a little green truck that he used to haul goods for the store and he *could* have taken us into some kind of country outside the big city, but he never did. There was always something to do at the store, even when it was closed, or he sat at home, frowning over his accounts.

Some of the girls at school were quite well off and had wonderful vacations. They even went to foreign countries like France or Switzerland. Miss Mayne, our geography teacher, said the next best thing to real traveling was "armchair traveling" and urged us to borrow travel books from the library. I did, of course, for I loved reading, and I wasn't really discontented, just a bit wistful sometimes.

When Adam was eleven he went to a school camp, but he said he hated every minute of it.

"It rained all the time, and the tents leaked, and there were cows all over the place. Mr. Crewe said it was an excellent chance to learn about trees and flowers and things, and he made us make lists. But they all looked the same to me. What do people *do* in the country?" Adam had asked Mother, when he came home.

"Work, mostly," Mother retorted. "And you have to have eyes to see. Once, believe it or not, I knew a lot. I made a collection of wild flowers. And trees . . . I knew them all."

Mother wasn't born in Liverpool. When she was

young she'd lived in a small town in the Midlands, and she spent several enchanted summers on a farm called Guelder Rose Farm in Oxfordshire. There was a tree called guelder rose, and the people who owned the farm where mother stayed were suitably named Farmer. They were family friends, and mother's own mother, when she was young herself, had known Guelder Rose Farm.

That was how we came to hear of Hunger Moss, because that great eerie stretch of country was near the farm. There was a ruined road the Romans might have made nearly two thousand years before, with an ancient tower in the very middle of it. And Mother had had a friend, a boy called Reuben, who had always come to meet her in their secret place until, one day, he had never come again.

Oh, it was all fascinating, like a fairy tale, but I had hardly thought about it for a long time. Then there came a day, in the summer of 1939, when, for no reason at all, I suddenly remembered Hunger Moss. It was a very hot day and I was unhappy, because there was family trouble. Not the usual trouble of big bills to be paid and the store doing badly because people in the area were too poor to spend much money. This was quite different. Adam had disgraced himself by getting into bad company, and Mother might have to have an operation.

It was late July and school had closed. I was alone in the house and I felt restless and miserable. My special friend, Jenny, was on vacation with her family in North Wales, and . . . well, everything seemed awful. I couldn't settle to anything, not even to reading the books I had borrowed from the library that morning. I knew I should get a meal ready for when Mother came home from the hospital and Dad closed the store, but I didn't even start doing that.

I wandered around the house, then ended up in my little bedroom. I stood there, staring at myself in the mirror. I was slim and dark haired, with large gray eyes, and I remember that I was very pale. There was a picture of Mother when she was about fourteen and I was very like her, though it had been taken in 1919 and her hair was long. It was because I was thinking of Mother as a girl that I remembered Hunger Moss. For a strange moment I seemed to see it shimmering in the heat, and Mother (or me) going across it on the half-lost Roman track.

I turned and looked out my window and there was Green Street with its old brick houses, and the vision was gone.

I ran down the stairs, opened the front door, and walked out into the intense heat of late afternoon. Green Street was a very convivial kind of place, especially on warm days, and the women were standing on their doorsteps or gathered in little groups on the sidewalk. I felt oddly conspicuous as I walked toward Smithdown Road. I had always been very happy there, but it was an aggressively respectable street and, since a policeman had brought Adam home, I'd been conscious that the gossip was sometimes about us.

Some of the women greeted me as I passed them. "Hello, Alice, love! All on your own? Where's that friend of yours?"

"She's gone to Wales." Jenny didn't belong to Green Street but they knew her because she was often with me. I walked on but I could hear some of the comments they made.

"Awful about her brother! Might have been in real trouble. Such a good boy, I'd have said. Shows you never can tell when kids get into bad company."

"If you ask *me* the trouble started when Adam didn't get a scholarship. His dad was real mad at him. That boy isn't stupid. Just lazy. Mr. Baker's ambitious for his children. Wants them to have a good education. And Alice is getting it."

I walked more slowly, curious to hear more. They were right about Adam. He'd been a fool and not worked. Then, when the result had come a few weeks ago, he'd abandoned the boys he knew and got in with a tough gang. It seemed that the whole street had witnessed his homecoming two days earlier.

The next group I came to were busy talking. "Now he'll have to leave school when he's fourteen and go out to work."

"Help his dad in the shop, most like."

They stopped talking when they saw me and called out various greetings as I went by. I walked along

13

slowly, thinking about it. If your parents weren't able to pay for your education, you had two choices. The one that was now Adam's fate—though not really his *choice* —or that of working hard enough to earn a free place at a secondary school. That was what I'd done, because I'd always known I had to get properly educated. I had a hope that one day I'd be able to go to a university.

Dad had been disappointed over Adam's failure, and he was dreadfully angry when he saw his son brought home in disgrace. The gang had been caught stealing from a stall in a street market. Although Adam hadn't been helping, he had been standing near, watching. A kindly local policeman, who knew him by sight, had brought him home. To make everything worse, Adam hadn't been repentent.

"I *wasn't* stealing," he said crossly. "I told them not to. But it was exciting to watch."

"Exciting!" Dad had stormed. "The next thing you'd have been doing it yourself. I never expected a boy of mine to disgrace us in front of the whole street."

Dad had forbidden Adam to see his new friends again, but Adam was growing up, he was in a contrary mood, and Liverpool was a tough place. He could go the right way or the wrong way. We had always been a very close family, but there were temptations all the time for boys with too much energy and not enough to do during the long vacation.

My head was starting to ache just with thinking. Smithdown Road was very hot, dusty, and noisy with traffic. Streetcars thundered up and down, and there were cars and trucks. Public houses stood on almost every corner, and on the corner where I had paused, a huge, horse-drawn wagon was loaded with beer barrels.

"Hey up, love!" a man shouted, rolling a barrel past me.

I crossed to the other corner. I wished I could get on a streetcar and go down to the pier head by the River Mersey, where it might be cooler. I glanced to my right toward Dad's store, which was the fourth one down. It was almost five-thirty and Dad had already taken in the sidewalk display of vegetables. He'd be home soon. He would be anxious if Mother hadn't come home from the hospital.

The shop nearest to me was a news agent's, and outside it there was an array of posters. One said in huge letters: "Hitler. . . . Latest."

Hitler. Germany. War. In spite of the heat I felt suddenly chilled. I tried not to think of the possibility of war, for after all it hadn't happened last year. They had dug trenches in the parks, and everyone had said war was imminent, but Mr. Chamberlain, the Prime Minister, had come back from an important meeting waving a piece of paper, some kind of treaty. He had said there would be peace, and he should know.

Suddenly I saw Adam coming toward me. He looked very hot. His dark hair was sticking to his forehead and he had torn his old shirt.

"Hello, Allie!" he said. "Why're you waiting here?"

15

"I was hoping someone would come," I answered. "Mother isn't back yet." But at that very moment I saw Mother getting off a streetcar. It was such a relief to see her that I felt better at once. You never knew with hospitals.

Mother was small and dark and rather pretty, but just then she looked tired and pale. I ran forward. "How did you get on?"

"I'm to go in next week . . . Wednesday. And they'll operate that day," Mother explained. "Don't look like that, Allie. I'm not having my leg off."

"No, I know," I said. "It's only your toe they're straightening or something." But it was alarming, all the same. No one in our family had ever had surgery.

"You and Adam go ahead and have the kettle boiling. I'll follow at my own pace."

I felt guilty because the meal wasn't ready. That came of looking in the mirror and dreaming of Hunger Moss. I seized Adam's hand and we ran down Green Street to Number Nineteen. I was thankful that most of the women had gone indoors. Some of the houses in Green Street were very small, in rows, with front doors opening onto the sidewalk. But at the far end they were bigger, with fences and gates, and tiny paved patches where some people tried to grow things in pots, though with little success. Ours was one of the bigger houses.

Adam cut bread, very thick, while I put on the kettle and brought out salad and cold meat. Then I washed four lovely ripe pears Dad had brought home from the store at one o'clock. I arranged them on a blue dish and wished I could paint. There was a bloom on them as they lay in a shaft of sunlight. Anything was better than thinking about being without Mother.

Adam was frowning and said nothing. He was really very unapproachable and I hated it, because we had always been quite close.

"I'll make the tea," I said. "They'll be here in no time." The kitchen was hot and I felt rather sick.

I went to the front door and looked out, and Mother and Dad were approaching together. Dad was saying, "Don't worry, Mary. It will all work out."

"Won't it cost an awful lot?" I asked anxiously, for I knew that people were afraid to be sick.

"No, we don't have to worry about that," Mother said. "It's lucky we paid that little insurance for so many years. They'll even send me to a Convalescent Home afterward."

We started the meal rather silently. In spite of the heavy gold of the sunlight striking the backyard wall and the yellow nasturtiums that climbed up the bricks, I had the feeling that everything around me was gray. Mother away from home . . . the long, empty weeks stretching ahead. What could we *do?* Adam had to be kept out of trouble, but how? I quite liked helping in the store, but Adam hated it. He particularly disliked delivering orders and Dad would expect him to do that. When Jenny came home I could go to her house, and there was always reading. But . . .

I caught Adam's eye and we looked at each other speculatively. I saw a similar glance between Dad and Mother, then Mother said, "Well, Bill, shall we tell them?"

"May as well," Dad agreed, chewing lettuce.

My stomach gave a kind of leap and I wasn't hungry. Was it more bad news? But Mother was smiling.

"We've fixed something wonderful," she said. "So you two needn't look so miserable. You've never had a proper holiday, Allie, love . . . time you did. That rainy camp didn't count, did it, Adam? Do you remember the Farmers?"

Adam looked completely blank, but I caught the implication of the capital letter and knew instantly that Mother meant those people at Guelder Rose Farm.

"That place in the country?" I asked. "Guelder Rose Farm. Yes, I remember. I was thinking about it today."

"You're both going there," Mother said. "Next week . . . Wednesday. How's that for a nice surprise?"

Oh, it was a surprise all right, but in the circumstances not a welcome one, even to me. My immediate thought was that we couldn't go *anywhere* when Mother was going into the hospital. A few minutes before I had been wondering how to pass the time, but suddenly I knew that of course I'd have to look after the house and go to visit Mother. There was no faintest possibility of going to that remote farm that belonged in a kind of fairy tale.

I tried to say what I was feeling, but Mother laughed.

"Look, my operation is quite a simple one. I'll be there about a week, then I'm going to a Convalescent Home for two weeks, because I won't be able to walk much at first. It's a nice place just outside Liverpool. Your dad will visit me, and he's going to stay with his brother in Anfield."

"But . . ."

"I wrote to the Farmers as soon as I heard I might have to go to hospital and they replied by return mail. I've always kept in touch with them. My mother did until she died; then . . . well, I never forgot them. They know all about you. They've often asked us there but, what with the store, and you and Adam being too young to go alone, it didn't happen."

"But now you are old enough," Dad chipped in. "And your Mother wants you to get to know that place. Learn things."

"It's no life for young people here in the city in summer," Mother said. "Things were so different for me when I was young."

The nasturtiums were swaying, melting together, and I blinked to try to steady them. Adam took a too large gulp of tea and choked most dramatically. His face went red and his eyes streamed, but when he could speak he said, "But you know I hated the country! I won't go. It's just to punish me, and I don't call it fair. What's Allie done that she's being punished, too?"

"Oh, don't be so silly!" Mother said sharply. "If you can think of the country as punishment it's high time you learned differently. Though we don't deny that you'll be better away from bad friends just now. I don't want you to hate the country, and you couldn't hate South Guelder." A dreamy look came into her eyes; the kind of look she used to have when she told us the stories. "I was fourteen, almost fifteen, when I saw it last. The Farmers must be getting old, but they love children."

"I'm not a child," I said. "And Adam may be only just twelve, but he's nearly as tall as I am."

"Well, young people, then," Mother said impatiently.

The thought of Mother as a girl of fourteen had an unreal quality. I just couldn't believe that we were going to that dream place; the great moss with the ruined tower, or castle. I only remembered bits of her stories, but I knew that Hunger Moss might be dangerous if you didn't know the right way across it.

"Why didn't you go back any more?" I asked.

Mother frowned, remembering. "I went first when I was nine, then every year. It was wartime, you know, and I suppose that added to the pleasure of it. Mrs. Farmer always said she'd fatten me up, because there was no shortage of butter, cheese, and home-cured ham on the farm. Well, I didn't know when it was the last time, but things happened. Mrs. Farmer was ill for a long while; then I left school and got a job. I met your father when he came down to our town to stay with some cousins, and we were married when I was nineteen. Since then . . . you know how it was, with the store and everything." After a pause she added, "It's just twenty years since I was in South Guelder."

"There never was much money," Dad said grimly, and he had that look on his face that always made me uneasy and sad. He'd had a hard boyhood, and he certainly knew nothing about the country. I thought maybe he sympathized with Adam, but he surprised me by going on, "Your mother says we're all missing things. Perhaps she's right."

And there in the hot kitchen, with the nasturtiums wavering against the brick wall outside, I felt as if I saw my parents for the first time. Dad, with his worn, kind face, and Mother, hot and tired, but still pretty. I believe, until then, I had taken them utterly for granted, but suddenly I knew that they were two separate people, who had had different beginnings, then come together and produced us. It was a startling moment; a real revelation.

The nasturtiums were still not very steady. Maybe a wind was rising; one of those eerie, thunder winds.

"Anyway, it's all fixed, so don't argue," Mother said. "There's a through train from Birkenhead Woodside Station, and you'll be met in Oxford."

"But how long will we be there?" I asked.

"You'll stay for several weeks," Mother answered.

2 The Lonely Place

We had never been anywhere by train, so it would be exciting. Adam admitted that, when we had a chance to talk alone. He looked hot, cross and tough, with his untidy hair, sweaty face, and torn shorts, but I knew him well enough to guess that he was scared by the very thought of the farm.

"There'll be cows," he said, "and I'll be expected to help. Well, I won't!"

"Cows don't hurt," I said uncertainly. Mother's stories had never included cows, but Adam was right and there would probably be dozens. Cows had to be milked, though I only knew how it was done from films and pictures in books. There were such things as milking machines, but not always, and it did look rather frightening, getting so close to those great beasts.

It was a strange evening, for, in our hitherto safe house, I suddenly had a feeling of impermanency. Mother rushed into a burst of activity and went through our clothes, most of which were very shabby. Only my school clothes were good; a navy-blue blazer and two dark-blue cotton dresses that were our summer uniform. Otherwise I only possessed two thin dresses, one green and one pink, some old shorts, and a few blouses.

We had strong shoes, much scuffed, and two pairs each of old sandals.

"You'll need the shoes," Mother said. "It does rain, and the Moss . . . you must be careful of the Moss."

"Hunger Moss," I said. It seemed incredible that we were going to see it.

"That's what they call it. Sometimes Hunger Moor, but it's really a kind of marsh. I did hear it had another name once, but people changed it. From the Latin or something; a name the Romans gave it."

After a pause, she continued dreamily, "I got to know the Moss well. Reuben and I knew the old road that goes across, two miles. He lived on the other side, in North Guelder. We made a map. Reuben was clever with maps. I don't remember now what became of it."

I waited. Mother reached up to bring some dusty, shabby suitcases from the top of a cupboard. Adam was lounging near us, silent with doubt.

"Reuben came every year, too, to Barleylands Farm. We were friends . . . I've told you. We had a secret place in the ruined tower. No one ever went there but us. That last summer, he came as usual. Then, after a few days, he never came again. I waited, and in the end I learned that his father and mother had come and taken him away. His father had a new job, very suddenly. They went to Scotland or somewhere . . . and he didn't even say goodbye."

I had heard it before, but until then I never realized the tragedy of it. I saw my mother—young, with long dark hair—waiting in a tower in a lonely place for a boy who did not come.

"Didn't you ever hear from him?"

"Not a word. It was as if he had died. I knew he hated writing letters, but still he did have my home address. Oh, I do want you both to go there, but do be careful! Hunger Moss . . . they said it waited for people who were unaware . . . was hungry for them. But we *knew* the Moss. It was ours, and I was never scared of it."

"Where was the secret place in the tower?" Adam asked.

"It was really a small castle." Mother began dusting the suitcases. "They said it had been a Roman station or something, then a castle, defending that part of the countryside. We had a room where we kept our things, but no doubt someone found it long ago. Though local folk were really afraid of the Moss; they said it was haunted."

Finally it was bedtime, but I was so scared, excited, and upset that I couldn't sleep. We were going to that lost, remote countryside where our mother had found happiness and, just possibly, heartache. When I heard footsteps on the landing I called out, and Mother came in.

"Aren't you asleep yet, Allie? It's ten-thirty. We'll be going to bed soon."

"Were you in love with Reuben?" I asked.

"At fourteen? What an idea! In 1919 girls of that age didn't talk about being in love. You girls of 1939 see too many films."

"Well, but you know it's possible," I argued. "Juliet was only fourteen, or was it thirteen? And some of the girls at my school say they're in love with older boys."

"I hope *you* don't." Mother sat on the edge of my bed. "I liked Reuben, anyway. That's all I thought it was. *He* was only fifteen. I did believe I knew him well enough to think he wouldn't go away without telling me, but he did, so I must have been wrong."

When she left me I lay there wakefully, thinking about Reuben and wondering why he had done that out-of-character, hurtful thing so long ago.

I slept for a while, then awoke feeling very hot and restless. Thunder was rumbling far away, and there really was a wind this time, moving the curtains. And, in those moments of awakening, I suddenly saw something strange in Mother's story . . . a fact I had never noticed before. She had waited and waited and had finally heard that Reuben had gone away, but why hadn't she gone straight across the Moss to Barleylands Farm in search of Reuben? Why just wait?

I was so thirsty, I got up and started to get a drink of water. As I crept along the landing, I heard voices from my parents' room.

"It's probably a very good idea in the circumstances," Dad was saying. Their door was a few inches open and his voice was clear. I froze, not wanting to be heard, not really meaning to listen.

"Yes," Mother answered. "If war does come, they may *have* to go away, Liverpool being an important

26

port and all that. This will get them used to being away from home . . ."

I turned and went back to bed, forgetting my thirst. Although it was so very hot, I was shivering. *Mother* . . . Mother believed there was going to be a war and that Liverpool would be bombed. At my school before the holidays there had been talk of plans for evacuation to North Wales. I don't think anyone in my class had taken it seriously. I had just tried not to know.

At last I fell deeply asleep and, in the morning, I thought I might have dreamed that overheard conversation.

After breakfast Mother didn't seem to want to talk about Hunger Moss, the castle, and her friendship with Reuben. "Some things don't concern you," she said. "Now you're going to the farm, I rather wish I hadn't talked so much about the Moss. I really thought you'd have forgotten my stories."

"I only remember bits of what you told us," I said. "But you can't expect us not to be interested. Adam will want to find that secret room, and so do I. But I'll see we don't get into any danger." Then I went on, "Why didn't you just go and look for Reuben when he didn't turn up that day?"

We were alone together in the kitchen, with the back door wide open to catch what air there was. The storm had never really broken, and it was another hot morning.

Mother looked at me in a startled kind of way, holding a dripping plate in her hand. "Well, I couldn't. I never went to Barleylands Farm."

"Why not? He must have gone to your farm."

"No, he never came to Guelder Rose. We always met on the Moss. You see, the Careys of Barleylands. . . . Oh, forget it, Allie! It's far in the past. I've almost forgotten myself." But I didn't really believe she had; those distant summers had been very important to her. "As for not getting into danger, Hunger Moss is a big area, with villages all around the outside of it. The first year I was there, the Farmers' son, Henry, taught me all about the Moss. He showed me all the boggy parts and put the fear of God in me about getting lost in mist. I was nine and Henry was fifteen and he probably found it boring, but he did a thorough job. I never once got lost, though the Roman track wasn't very clear then."

"Perhaps it's gone now," I said regretfully. Twenty years was a very long time.

"Maybe it has," Mother agreed. "It went pretty straight, for that's the way the Romans built roads, but part of it had sunk and you had to go around the bad patches. You had to know what to look for—stones and bushes and the like. Few people ever walked across; if they wanted to go to North Guelder they cycled or walked around the Moss. Not many people had cars then, though the Farmers had a trap. I was quite good with the pony." She sounded surprised by her long-ago skill.

28

"But we aren't nine," I pointed out. "I'm sensible, I hope."

"You're only used to city streets, though. If the Farmers tell you not to go, you listen to them, and make Adam listen, too. There'll be plenty to see around the edge. Henry's married and gone, so he can't help you as he did me. Then, of course, after I met Reuben, Henry washed his hands of me."

"But I thought Reuben lived on the other side of Hunger Moss," I said. "So you had to go alone to meet him."

"Yes, I went alone." Mother frowned. "I was there for several weeks, for six summers. Don't rush things, anyway. The Farmers will very likely keep you both busy on the farm. Two more pairs of hands are sure to be welcome in the fields this time of year, and Adam's strong for his age. Best thing for him will be if he's kept hard at work. And there'll be chickens and pigs to look after, as well as calves and—"

"Cows," I said, thinking of Adam. He might be twelve years old and strong, but I understood my brother pretty well and he always told me more than he told our parents. He really had developed a deep fear of cows during that summer at camp, because a bad-tempered one had chased a boy who fell and broke his arm. The master in charge had said it hardly ever happened; you just got the odd beast like that. But, after all, there'd be bulls, too, and they must be worse. I knew there were going to be problems at Guelder

Rose Farm even before Mother said, "Yes, they have a large milking herd. I was quite a good milker, but I liked working in the fields better. When I wasn't with Reuben I often helped with the harvest. They grew oats and wheat and a field or two of barley. I loved the barley before it was cut, so tall and silvery. There was a path through the middle, and there were poppies and cornflowers . . . " She stood there staring at the dirty dishwater, lost in country memories, and I felt suddenly cut off from her, unable to share. That was really why she wanted us to go, because there was a whole world we didn't understand.

And I wondered suddenly how happy she had been in a house in a narrow city street, even though she had the three of us and we had always seemed such a close family. Perhaps some part of her had died when she no longer could go to Guelder Rose Farm and walk through the growing barley or out across Hunger Moss to meet Reuben. I *must* be growing up, for I was having such strange thoughts, and I wasn't sure I liked them.

But Mother was herself again, the remote look gone.

"Anyway, just you be careful. A few people did go to Hunger Moss, walkers and the like, though it's not a place that would draw many tourists. The villages aren't special, like others in Oxfordshire. I hope I've done the right thing, but the Farmers will look after you."

I knew then I hadn't dreamed that conversation overheard in the night, and I opened my mouth to ask her if she really believed there would be war. But the words never came out, because I was afraid to hear her answer. We were going to South Guelder just for a holiday, and there *couldn't* be war.

As the days passed Adam grew more sulky and difficult, and I was in a churn of excitement and vague fear. Fear of Mother in hospital, and of our coming journey to a strange world, with unknown people. If we didn't like the Farmers, or they didn't like us, it would be dreadful; and it was going to be difficult for them to like Adam in his present mood.

The old suitcases, so long unused, were packed. The only new things we had were raincoats, very strong, but thin.

"Thank goodness you don't need fancy clothes on a farm," Mother said. "You can travel in your school things."

A third suitcase was packed for her to take to the hospital, and I kept glancing at it uneasily, but Mother seemed quite cheerful about the whole thing and said she'd at least have a good rest.

"You're not to worry about me," she said to us on Tuesday evening. "Write if you have time. It's Ward 8, and you have the Anfield address. Just enjoy yourselves and learn all you can."

Wednesday was rather dark and cloudy, but still warm. I couldn't eat much breakfast, though I hoped Mother hadn't noticed. I helped to pack up sandwiches, cake, and fruit, with two bottles of lemonade, and thought I would probably feel hungry when we were on the train. But it was awful saying goodbye to Mother. If *only* she were coming with us, and we could all three walk through barley fields and cross the Moss together.

Dad drove us in the van through the Mersey Tunnel to Birkenhead Woodside Station. He bought the tickets and gave them to me, and he bought comics for Adam and a school-girl magazine for me to read during the journey. I'd stopped reading such things a year or two ago, but Dad had evidently never noticed. Dad had no feeling for books, and he actually thought reading a waste of time. As we followed him down the long train, my thoughts curiously made me more fond of him. He looked so worn and anxious, and I knew he was in a desperate hurry to get back to the shop. I really must be growing up; I wanted to protect him from unhappiness.

There were boards all along the train with place names in huge letters. In the end it would arrive at Paddington, London. But we were to get off at Oxford. My troubled fondness for Dad changed to a hot, cross feeling when he put us into a compartment already occupied by a middle-aged woman wearing a bright pink hat. He found out she was going as far as Oxford and asked her if she would look after us and see that we got off there.

"Just stand on the platform," Dad told us, for about the tenth time. "Mr. Farmer will meet you."

"We'll be all right," I replied, though I suddenly

wanted to cry. For him? For myself, because I was nearly fourteen and had never made a train journey before? I added hurriedly, "Goodbye, Dad! You get to the shop. Let us know about Mother."

Dad kissed me, patted Adam on the shoulder, and jumped out of the train. He hurried away without looking back.

Ten minutes later the train started with tremendous belches of steam from the great engine, and we went through a tunnel into the gray daylight beyond.

The woman in the pink hat wanted to be talkative and asked questions about where we were going and what schools we went to, but, getting little response, she turned to her paper. Adam read his comics and I sat staring out the windows, lost in dreams. It seemed utterly unbelievable that we would see Guelder Rose Farm and Hunger Moss that very day.

After Birmingham the sun began to shine and the summer countryside was bathed in brilliant light. There were streams overhung with willows after we left Banbury, and fields where oats, wheat, and barley were growing high and golden. Our fellow traveler in the pink hat turned out to be useful, after all, for she lived in the country and told me the names of things. She seemed so astonished that I knew nothing at all about it that I felt ashamed and hopelessly lacking in vital knowledge. She said it was going to be an early harvest, and in some fields the oats were already being cut. Adam showed some interest in the reaper and binder, but I saw his face change every time we passed a field of cows.

"You know, Allie," he said, as we stood out in the corridor to stretch our legs, "I do hate those animals. I'm scared of them, and that's the truth. In Liverpool I'm never scared of anything, and I think it's a rotten mean trick to punish me by sending me to this place for weeks on end."

"Oh, don't be a fool!" I said crossly, glancing sideways at his hot face. "It isn't a punishment. It would be wonderful if only Mother wasn't in hospital, and *you* weren't such a nuisance. Why can't you try and enjoy yourself? Not," I added honestly, "that I'm keen on the idea of cows myself. They *are* so big."

"I'll kill you if you tell anyone I'm scared, Allie!"

"I won't tell. It'll be our secret." But I was terribly afraid it wouldn't remain a secret for long, once we reached the farm.

Oxford seemed quite a way from Banbury. I was silent again and let my mind drift. It was unkind of Mother not to tell her stories again before we left, but everything she had ever said must be somewhere in my mind. The quickly passing scene and the bright light had a hypnotic effect, and a few more facts floated up, like dead goldfish in a bowl. Reuben had red hair and freckles and was not handsome. He had a whistle and used to play tunes. If he was at the meeting place first, he would pipe to her as she crossed the Moss. A mouth organ would have seemed more natural. Boys always had harmonicas, and Adam made an awful noise with his.

As clearly as if it had happened to me, I could see the boy standing high on the tower, the whistle to his lips. There was an old man who played one on Smithdown Road, hoping for money.

A jolt brought me back to the hot, crowded train, and a platform began to slide past. I went back into the compartment and grabbed my coat, raincoat, and one of the suitcases. Adam took the other, and we stumbled after the woman in the pink hat.

We had only just stepped out of the train when an old man wearing a shabby suit of thick tweed came up to us and asked, "You the Bakers? Good! I'm Bert Farmer." His voice was deep and slow and I liked his face at once, but he seemed very old to me. I learned later that he was sixty-five.

He took my suitcase and led the way out of the station, to where a shabby old Ford was parked. I was almost surprised that it wasn't a pony and trap. The back seat was partly occupied by two sacks of chicken feed, and I took the remaining space, while Mr. Farmer stowed away the luggage. Adam sat in front.

Mr. Farmer didn't talk much until Oxford was left behind, and even then there was a good deal of traffic. There was no sign of remote countryside. I studied Mr. Farmer's back. He had broad, strong shoulders and thick, grizzled hair, while his neck and face were reddish brown. He looked reassuringly kind and comfortable.

We came to a sign that said: SOUTH GUELDER 5 MILES
. . . EAST MARSHLAND 7 MILES . . . WEST MARSHLAND
7 MILES.

"Those are all villages on the south side of the Moss,"
Mr. Farmer said, swinging the car onto the much narrower, quieter road. Suddenly we were in deep summer countryside. The hedges were hung with honeysuckle, traveler's joy, and late wild roses, and the banks
were a waving mass of foxgloves, high grasses, and
ferns. I didn't know any of the names then, but I noted
every detail so that I had them in my mind forever, and
I gradually learned their names. It was like waking up
after being deeply asleep, that journey to Guelder Rose
Farm.

All the growing things were swaying in a hot breeze.
The car windows were open and my hair blew into my
eyes. I breathed in the enchanted, warm fragrance of
the air. Air never smelled like that in Liverpool; it was
like being drowned in a scented bath.

Once we were driving along in peace, Mr. Farmer
asked a few questions and Adam did most of the an-
swering, though in a slightly surly fashion. I was glad I
had chosen the back seat and could dream, lost in a
vision of greenness and flowers. Mother must have
come this way all those years ago, to her beloved place.

The countryside had seemed very flat, but suddenly
the road wound, each bend taking it higher. At the top
Mr. Farmer stopped the car and I looked ahead and to
the right. Adam's shoulders had been hunched but now

they straightened. At the foot of the hill lay a tiny village. There was a church built of pale gold stone, with a stone Vicarage close by, a few cottages, and, a little apart, a farmhouse and farm buildings.

"South Guelder," Mr. Farmer said. "And that's my farm."

I was astonished that South Guelder was so small, but it was the view beyond the village that caught and held my attention. It was a curious stretch of countryside, almost circular, with the land rising slightly all around. Away on the other side, I could see another village in the clear afternoon light.

I knew that I was looking at Hunger Moss. There were no fields in the Moss; there were bushes and a few trees and patches of golden stone here and there. There was a lot of very bright grass, or it looked like grass at that distance, and in the middle, a little to the left, rose a big ruined building. There was a broken tower, and walls, and black gaps that must be windows.

Across the very center of the Moss, starting close to South Guelder, was a kind of line. Not a real road, nothing as clear as that; just a suggestion of a track. Here and there the grass was darker, and there was a grayish patch near the middle that looked like a bit of causeway. But that was a mile away and near the castle.

"What a lonely place!" I said softly, breaking the silence. "Hunger Moss!"

3 We Venture onto Hunger Moss

"You've heard about the Moss, have you?" Mr. Farmer asked. "I expect your mother told you. She loved it. She loved the whole place. It's a long time ago, but I remember that last time she went away. Of course she didn't know then it was her last visit. 'Mr. Farmer,' she said, 'every time I go away I leave a bit of myself behind.' "

I had thought that maybe part of her had died, deprived of the farm and Hunger Moss, but I'd been wrong. That part of her was here still. The scene floated, dreamlike, in front of the sudden mist in my eyes. How silly to want to cry, but it seemed so sad. Mrs. Baker, who lived in Green Street and helped in a shop on Smithdown Road. My mother, who had been a child here, happy and free. No one could ever be free in Green Street; you had to conform, and work hard, and forget dreams.

"We're going to get to know Hunger Moss," Adam said, with more than a trace of truculence, and I put my hand warningly on his shoulder.

Mr. Farmer began to drive slowly down the hill. "The Moss isn't to be trifled with," he said.

We came to a crossroads, where the right-hand road

went to East Marshland and the one on the left to West Marshland. Straight ahead, narrower than before, the road led to South Guelder. A sign said: NO THROUGH ROAD. On one corner was a small cottage, with a long, low building attached. The building had wide-open doors and I could see the hindquarters of a big cart horse. There was a clanging sound and a strange smell in the air. Far back in the gloom was the glow of a furnace.

A big red-faced man was leaning against the wall, but he came forward when Mr. Farmer stopped the car. "This is my carter and waggoner," Mr. Farmer said. "Tom Barlow. One of the horses went lame. Ever seen a forge before?"

"No."

Tom Barlow leaned right into the car. "You got the children all right?" He grinned at us and he had a front tooth missing. "Jim'll be glad of their company. Not that the lad has much time now school's closed and he's in the fields all day. Going to help, are you?"

"Give 'em a chance," Mr. Farmer said quickly. "City children; not used to the country. But after a few days . . . "

"Girl's the spittin' image of her mother," Mr. Barlow said, staring at me. "Well I'm remembering Mary Selby."

I'd somehow forgotten that other people would remember Mother besides the Farmers. But Mr. Farmer was starting the car again. "Get back soon as you can,

Tom," he was saying. "Plenty to do."

South Guelder, crouching so small and lost at the edge of Hunger Moss, really seemed like the end of the world. Maybe Mr. Farmer guessed some of our feelings for he said, "Must seem strange to you both, coming from a big city. You're far too pale, to my mind. Your mother never had that city look, but Tom's right. You're your mother over again, Alice."

The tiny main street of the village had four stone cottages on either side, a very small inn covered in creeper and roses with a sign, THE HUNGER ARMS, and a slightly larger cottage near the church gate that was the general store and post office. There was no one in sight, though I saw some curtains twitch. A ginger cat was asleep on a wall, and a small black dog barked as we passed.

"Has everyone died?" Adam asked in an aggressive voice. His shoulders were hunched again and all my uneasiness returned. He had been interested in our first sight of Hunger Moss, but now we were near the farm. . . . I rushed in hastily with another question: "Isn't there a school?"

"There are only seven children," Mr. Farmer explained. "Four of school age and three babies. The elder ones go to school in East Marshland."

The road dropped slightly toward Hunger Moss. It ceased to be a proper road close to the farm but went on as a rutted, grass-grown track. The way to Hunger Moss!

41

The farmyard was full of black-and-white cows, and a tall young man with untidy fair hair was driving them into a long stone building. It must be milking time. I could hear the clatter of buckets.

"We don't have to go that way," I whispered to Adam, as Mr. Farmer stopped the car and told us to get out.

A green-painted side gate opened into a garden full of flowers, and a path led to the door of the farmhouse. The house was built of the lovely golden stone and had gables, chimneys that looked very old, and a roof of russet tiles, overgrown here and there with moss. I think I fell in love with Guelder Rose Farm at that moment, as my mother might have done when she arrived there at the age of nine. The past kept stabbing me with something like memory, as if it had been I who came there once in a pony and trap, my long dark hair swinging.

A woman came hurrying out of the house; she was plump and white haired and she wore a blue dress and a clean white apron. While Mr. Farmer unloaded the chicken feed and our suitcases, she opened the gate and came up to us. She kissed me, then Adam, who flinched. Adam hated being kissed. His eyes were still on the cows.

"How are you, my dears?" Mrs. Farmer cried. "Welcome to Guelder Rose Farm. It's a happy day for us. I always wanted to see Mary's children."

We walked up the garden path, safe from the cows.

The sun was hot and the air so sweet that I wanted to breathe and breathe, to make sure I made the best of it. The house was cool and rather dark, and we went along a stone-flagged passage to the kitchen. I gasped when I saw the room, because it looked so old. There were thick oak beams overhead and a huge inglenook fireplace, with stone seats on either side of where the fire would be on winter nights.

"Oh, Mrs. Farmer!" I cried. "It's like something in a book!"

She laughed heartily and switched on an electric kettle.

"There are plenty of kitchens like this around. You must see the one at East Marshlands Farm. There's a secret chamber in behind the inglenook. Now, you must be hungry. Sit you down, my dears, and set to."

The huge table was partly covered with a red-and-white cloth and there was a great deal of food. Thick slices of home-cured ham quite unlike the thin little slices we bought at a shop on Smithdown Road, meat pie with an egg in the middle, cold new potatoes, and the kind of lettuce and tomatoes Dad never sold in his shop. A big crusty loaf, an enormous dish of rich butter, and, to one side, a bowl of fresh raspberries and a jug of cream. There was also a fruit cake, scones, and jam.

"Oh, I say!" said Adam, gazing in astonishment at the laden table. I kicked him, because that wasn't polite, and he glared back. We sat down and Mr. Farmer came in. Mrs. Farmer poured out cups of very strong tea and the meal began. Mr. Farmer ate quickly, drank two cups of tea, and hurried away to help with the milking.

Mrs. Farmer plied us with food but didn't try to make us talk. Maybe she guessed how strange and homesick we felt. I hope she did, because otherwise we must have seemed very rude. It was all marvelous, the food and the kitchen and the beautiful old house in its glowing garden, but I couldn't help remembering home and how no one was there.

"Come up and see your rooms," Mrs. Farmer said, when we had finished. "You're having the room that used to belong to your mother, Alice."

"Oh, I'm so glad!" I said. By now, the operation must be over. I wished I hadn't eaten so much as we followed Mrs. Farmer to the old oak staircase that twisted and creaked and led to uneven hallways upstairs.

It was a lovely room and somehow it made me think of *Anne of Green Gables*. There was a gable, and the window looked straight into a huge old apple tree, and the tree was covered with apples. It was the first time I had ever seen apples growing, and when I told Mrs. Farmer she looked horrified.

"Never seen apples growing?"

"I don't think so, Mrs. Farmer," I said. "Dad sells them in the shop, but they come in boxes."

"Mary Selby's children!" she murmured, looking at me as if I came from the moon. "You should have come here years ago, love."

Adam's room was along the passage. It had old

beams, a tipsy floor, and looked out into the farmyard.

"I'll swop if you like," I said, when Mrs. Farmer had gone downstairs. Although I loved my room already, it seemed hard on Adam, in his present mood, to have a view of something he dreaded.

"Doesn't matter," he said crossly, staring at the cows being driven back to their pasture.

"But it does, if you hate it. Honestly . . . "

"Oh, go and unpack!" he said, and began to fling his clothes out of the old suitcase and into the drawers of a bureau. "I'm going to put on my old shorts, and my shirt with the patch."

"Good idea! I'll put on my pink dress." Our school clothes were too neat, and too precious, for a farm. I went slowly back to my room. The ancient boards creaked and there was a nice smell of polish and lavender. I unpacked, more tidily than Adam, and tried to eat an apple straight off the bough, but it wasn't ripe. There was a bookcase filled with children's books. When I had changed my dress I fell on my knees in front of it.

I pulled out *Little Women* and saw that "To Dear Mary from Maggie Farmer" was written on the flyleaf. Left there for another day that had never come. I gulped and saw the girl who had been there long ago kneeling where I was now. I felt haunted.

"Oh, good! Unpacked and taken off your good dress." Mrs. Farmer stood in the doorway, surprising me. "Then why don't you and your brother go out? But do be careful. We have to talk to you about the Moss. It's boggy in places. Just see the village now."

"Mother . . . knew Hunger Moss," I said.

"So she did. She knew the way across, but it must be fainter now. No one goes."

It was too early to fight for our right to get to know the Moss. We went out into the hot evening. The wind had dropped and the trees and grasses were motionless. The whole world smelled of roses. We walked through the green gate and turned our backs on the farmyard. To our right was the tiny village street, to our left the track that led to the Moss. We hesitated, looking one way, then the other.

"I don't want to see any more people," Adam said truculently.

"There aren't any people," I pointed out, for the street was empty. I knew what he wanted, and I wanted it, too; just to be near Hunger Moss.

Silently, guiltily on my part, we turned down the narrow, overgrown lane. The grasses, brambles, and flowers were high, and had encroached so much between the hedgerows that there was just room for us to walk side by side.

Before very long we came to a stile half buried in hedge parsley and ferns. Beyond was the Moss but, at that exciting moment, we heard the sound of whistling behind us and swung around to see who was coming. It was a boy about my age, big and brown haired, with sun-tanned face and arms. He was accompanied by the black dog we had seen earlier in the village.

"Saw you turn down here," he said. "I was just coming out of our cottage. You're the two who've come to stay at Guelder Rose Farm? I'm Jim Barlow. My dad said you'd arrived."

We eyed him cautiously, both of us resenting his presence. The Moss lay invitingly behind us, and it was just ill luck that the village hadn't been as empty as it had seemed.

"Oh, hello!" I said, since Adam didn't speak. "Yes, we've come to stay a while. I'm Alice Baker and this is Adam, my brother."

"From a city? Liverpool?" Jim seemed to find that amazing. "I was in Oxford last year."

"Last *year?*" I repeated, wondering if he was being funny, for Oxford wasn't far away. "Don't you mean last week?"

"No, I don't. I hate towns," said Jim. "In my holidays I work for Mr. Farmer. I like working in the fields. We live at Moss Cottage and my dad works for Mr. Farmer. I've two little sisters; one's six and the other's three. There's only one other boy in the village, Steve Brace, and he's eight. I don't suppose you know much about the country."

I glanced at Adam and saw he had gone rather red. Jim would be his only possible boy companion, and I wished they would get on, but doubted if they could.

Jim's tone implied that he would have little sympathy with towny ways, and he certainly couldn't know what it was like to be scared of cows.

"No, we don't know anything about the country," Adam said aggressively.

"But we want to learn," I added, turning to look over the stile toward Hunger Moss.

"You keep away from the Moss," Jim ordered sharply.

"Why?" I continued to stare at the scene before me. For a short distance there was a kind of path. There was gorse at the edge and the grass that had looked so green from above wasn't, perhaps, grass at all. Not ordinary grass . . . reeds? From that low point I couldn't see the castle, nor any of the scattered stones.

"Oh, no one goes there," Jim answered in an offhand voice. "There used to be a track all the way over, people say. One of those hikers with rucksacks had to be rescued, back in the spring. He went into the bog. Hunger Moss," he added laconically, "gets you."

"Why should it?" I asked over my shoulder. I wasn't going to tell Jim Barlow that the moor had been our mother's friend. That was our secret.

"Oh, it's a lostlike place. Haunted, they say."

"But . . . "

"If we want to go to North Guelder we drive around, or cycle," Jim said quickly.

I thought that maybe Jim was scared of Hunger Moss, and the idea was rather cheering. It seemed sillier to be afraid of a place than of a herd of cows. Adam may have had the same idea, for he said scornfully, "No one believes in ghosts. What ghosts, anyway?"

Jim laughed and said slowly in his deep country voice, "The Romans, perhaps. *They* made the track over the Moss, didn't they? It's all a lot of rot, but you'd better keep off." He turned and walked away. "See you later," he said over his shoulder. "Come on, Floss! Home!" And boy and dog disappeared around a slight bend.

His presence had broken the spell, reminding us that we had to contend with local people, but once he had gone and deep silence lay over everything again, we gazed at the Moss and found it desirable.

"He believed that about its being haunted," Adam said. "I'm going over the stile."

"But we oughtn't to," I argued. "It may not be haunted, but it is probably dangerous. And Mrs. Farmer said . . . "

But Adam was over the stile and I followed. The faint path was hard and there was a definite way through the bright green grass.

"Let me go first then," I said, and we changed places. Adam muttered, "It *is* a rum place! So quiet and lonely." And I guessed he was thinking of Smithdown Road and the other teeming streets of Liverpool.

The weather had been dry and my feet in old sandals found firm ground so easily that I soon grew overconfident. I walked rapidly between two twisted old bushes and found myself up to the knees in bog. I didn't sink any deeper, but the brown water had splashed the whole front of my dress, and, when I moved to try and step back, I nearly lost a sandal.

"Darn!" I shouted. I felt a whole series of emotions: Mrs. Farmer would be mad . . . Hunger Moss had "got" me . . . and I had spoiled my dress. I was annoyed with myself and apprehensive, for we would never be trusted again. So much for my promise to Mother that I would be sensible.

"Get me out of this!" I cried to Adam, who was laughing rather hysterically. It had been a long, strange day and he was out of his depth (though not in the way I was), and I really must have looked funny, standing there in the bog.

I tried to turn around to face him and nearly fell. Gone were dreams for the moment, and Hunger Moss seemed cold and uninviting.

I managed cautiously to turn, and Adam, still laughing, took my hands. I was dragged onto firm ground, still, luckily, wearing both sandals, though they were utterly sodden. My bare legs were brown, deeply stained by bog water.

"I do wish I hadn't been such an idiot!" I groaned, as we started back. "It's all your fault for climbing the stile."

"You look a fine mess!" my brother said unsympathetically.

We walked in silence through the hot, golden evening. The farmhouse gate was reached all too soon, and there was Mrs. Farmer in the garden. She shrieked when she saw me.

"There! I told you to see the village! That wretched moor . . . it's not safe. I thought you'd be a sensible girl, Alice."

I opened my mouth, then shut it again, for I didn't want to give Adam away. But Adam said, "It was my fault, not Allie's. I climbed the stile and she just came, too."

"But I wanted to go," I confessed. I had recovered myself a little. "I know it was rather silly to go so soon and I'm sorry. If I hadn't walked so fast I'd have seen the boggy bit. It seemed so dry at first. *Next* time we'll go slowly. We'll make a map, as Mother did. We *have* to know Hunger Moss, Mrs. Farmer."

"We'll see," Mrs. Farmer answered. "You'd better get into the bath and I'll wash your dress at once. That brown stuff will be hard to get out. And your sandals . . . what a mess! You can both go to bed, anyway. You've had a long day."

She led the way to the bathroom, which was huge, with low beams. Later I learned that it had been made out of a bedroom. The tub was very old-fashioned with curiously shaped legs and enormous brass taps. It stood on a low platform. I took off my dress while Mrs. Farmer ran hot water and produced a big, fluffy towel and a large cake of pink soap.

"Mary did make a map," she said. "She and that boy

Reuben. Very clever it was, with little pictures around it. She showed me once." She turned off the hot tap and ran some cold water. "I suppose," she added, "you're far too old for me to come back and scrub your legs?"

I looked at her kind face and knew she was wishing I was younger, as my mother had been when she first came to the farm. I didn't really mind being seen in the bath; Mother often came in while I was soaking.

"You can if you like," I said. "It's going to be hard to get them clean." She laughed and went away with my dress and the awful wet sandals.

The pink soap had a delicious smell and I lay and looked around the unusual bathroom. Ours at home was so tiny. The lavatory here stood on a little platform of its own, and the base was of blue-and-white patterned china. Outside the window was a pear tree. I could just see the top branches, with small green pears clinging to a bough.

If I hadn't been so worried about Mother and Adam I knew I could be very happy at Guelder Rose Farm. As for the Moss . . . violently I wished that I hadn't been so silly as to fall into the bog. For Hunger Moss drew me with a force that could not be denied.

4 What We Saw from the Church Tower

Mrs. Farmer came back and scrubbed my legs so hard that I almost yelled. It was most painful, but the brown stuff began to come off.

"We met Jim Barlow by the stile," I told her. "He said Hunger Moss is haunted. Is it?"

I looked at her face, hot and steamy as she bent over the tub, and somehow read her thoughts. She was thinking that if we were scared enough we would keep away from the Moss. But after a few moments she said, "Jim was teasing."

"Well, he seemed to mean it."

"Oh, folk will always talk," she said. "I don't know the Moss at all. I've spent a long married life here and never been over that stile. Forty years and never once . . . "

I stared at her unbelievingly, for it couldn't be true. The stile was only a very short distance away. *"You're teasing!"* I said.

"No, I'm not. I had no reason for going there. I'm not fond of walking for walking's sake. The things people say are just ignorance. I've never been conscious of being afraid of the place; I just haven't gone there. But my son Henry did. He has a farm of his own now, ten miles away. He knew Hunger Moss and taught your mother to respect it when she was just a little thing. Still, haunted or not, the moor's a dangerous place. I'll talk to Bert when he comes in. He's gone to the pub for his evening drink."

Scrubbed clean and in my pajamas, I knelt again to look at the books. There was a big atlas, a dictionary, and all kinds of stories. Some were boys' books, but others had Mother's name in them.

"She's going to ask Mr. Farmer about the Moss when he comes back from the pub," I told Adam, when he looked in to say good night.

"He'll stop us going there." Adam went to the window, picked an apple, and tried to drop it on a hen scratching the ground below. The hen made a loud protest and Adam laughed. "I hate the silence of this place," he said morosely, and went away.

I didn't hate it, but I did find the quiet strange and rather sad. The only sounds were the twittering of birds and the distant lowing of cows. At eight o'clock on a summer evening everyone in Green Street would be out on the doorsteps, the older people with chairs on the pavement, enjoying the company. And there would be the steady roar of traffic.

About thirty children and young people lived in Green Street and at least a dozen dogs. It was a convivial street, unaware of cows, or ghosts, or a place called Hunger Moss that swallowed you up.

When Mrs. Farmer came to say good night she held

an orange envelope in her hand. My heart did a queer leap at sight of it.

"Mrs. Cox from the post office has just brought this," she said cheerfully. "It's from your dad. He says: 'Operation over. Mother fine. Don't worry.'"

For a moment I wanted to cry, for I had never thought of Dad's sending an expensive telegram. Then relief flooded through me.

"Oh, now I can really enjoy being here!" I said.

Mrs. Farmer kissed me. "I hope you will, Alice, dear. Oh, my! You are so like your mother. It's just like having her back again. But what's the matter with your brother?"

"Adam?" I stared at her. "He's not used to the country. He'll be all right . . . later."

"Didn't he want to come?"

"Well, no-o. He went to the country once before, with his school, and he didn't like it."

"It wouldn't be like South Guelder," she said, with such certainty that I laughed. But I didn't feel like laughing when she went on. "Best thing for the boy will be to get to work along with Jim. Jim may say the Moss is haunted but he's sensible for all that, and a hard worker."

When she had gone I settled down, but I couldn't sleep. It was very hot and my thoughts went round and round. I needn't worry about Mother, but there was still Adam, and still the problem of Hunger Moss. In the end I got up again and leaned out the window. The birds sounded sleepy now, and there were so many sweet smells. It was beginning to grow dark.

I wondered if Adam were asleep and thought I'd go and look, very quietly. To reach his room I had to pass the top of the main stairs, and voices came up from below. I froze, remembering that other time at home when I had overheard a conversation. But if adults sent you to bed too early, then talked in loud voices, it was likely to happen.

"Must keep them away from Hunger Moss," Mr. Farmer said clearly. "Difficult, though."

Feeling no guilt at all, this time, I leaned on the oak stair rail and listened. If Hunger Moss was lost to me, I couldn't bear it.

"Too difficult," said Mrs. Farmer. "They've heard about it and they're interested. And it's not *really* dangerous. No one's sunk into the bog and never been seen again. I suppose it's easy to get lost in mist, but in fine weather. . . . There was that walker chap, though."

"He was wearing a heavy rucksack," said Mr. Farmer. "He only had a scare, anyway. But if someone could show them, that might make it all right. Maybe Henry would come. Write to him, Maggie, and ask him. And, in the meantime, maybe they'll get interested in the farm. We'll get them working. The girl can look for eggs and help to feed the calves." There was a silence. The scent of pipe smoke floated up to my nostrils. Mr. Farmer was lighting up and thinking.

"I'll tell 'em Hunger Moss is forbidden for the present," he said. "If this dry weather keeps on, it should be all the safer later."

"They won't like it. They want to go."

"Can't think what attracts them," Mr. Farmer said, rather grumpily. "Useless land, that's all it is, and always has been."

"Mary felt the same, and so did Henry."

"Well, I'll tell 'em and I'll break their necks if they disobey again."

I crept back to bed and quite soon I fell asleep. But I dreamed about Hunger Moss.

At five-thirty the next morning, the farmhouse stirred. At home we never got up before seven-thirty so I tried to go to sleep again, but it was impossible. There were heavy feet on the stairs, and then doors and gates opening, the lowing of cows, and a cock crowing loudly. If we had wanted noise we had it now, though such different sounds from Green Street. Someone was whistling; cans clanged. It must be even noisier in Adam's room.

I got up and went to see if he was awake. He was standing by his window, looking sleepy and cross. The farmyard was simply crammed with cows, enormous beasts, jostling each other as they made for the cowshed.

"Sure as fate," said Adam, "Mr. Farmer'll try to make me help. And I won't, Allie. I can't! I wish every single

57

cow was at the bottom of the bog. How often do they get milked?"

"You've been in the country before," I pointed out, for I had no idea. At least twice a day, it seemed. It was awful to be so ignorant, but how could one be anything else when our milk had come in bottles, or in our old china jug sometimes, if I just went to the dairy on Smithdown Road.

Adam went on, "I'm a coward, Allie, and everyone will know and laugh."

I was afraid that was true and could think of nothing comforting to say. I went back to bed and dozed a little. Mrs. Farmer called us at seven, and breakfast was at seven-thirty. By the time we went down I had told Adam about the conversation I'd overheard and he looked gloomier than ever. But he was fond of his food, and the breakfast was wonderful. Porridge with cream, home-cured bacon and fresh eggs, and as much toast, butter, and marmalade as we could hold.

Mr. Farmer ate quickly as seemed to be his habit. Dad always ate his breakfast quite slowly, reading the *Daily Mail* at the same time. But there was no newspaper in sight at Guelder Rose and I hadn't seen a wireless. I learned later that there was a very old set in the sitting room. There were piles of a magazine called *The Farmers' Weekly* in a corner of the kitchen and I never saw Mr. Farmer read anything else during the weeks that followed.

Some train of thought, perhaps the feeling that the

real and trouble-filled world was far away from that quiet old kitchen, made me ask suddenly, as Mr. Farmer wiped his mouth and rose to go back to work, "Mr. Farmer, do you think there'll be a war?"

It was Mrs. Farmer who answered. "A war, Alice? Bless my heart, I hope not! Mr. Chamberlain said there wouldn't be, didn't he, last year?"

"But—"

"You never can tell with those chaps in London." Mr. Farmer stumped to the door in his great boots. "Or with all those darned foreigners. Never trust Germans."

"It probably wouldn't affect us here, anyway," Mrs. Farmer said comfortably, pouring herself out a third cup of strong tea.

"Yes, it would, Maggie." Mr. Farmer paused with his hand on the door. "You can't have forgotten last time. They took most of the young men and we were hard put to it to get the work done until the two Land Girls came. They were fine girls and they worked as hard as any man, but we don't want to go through that again. This time they'd probably blow us sky high with bombs or something."

"The Germans have never heard of South Guelder," Mrs. Farmer said, still quite comfortably.

"Well, we'll worry about it if it comes. I've got to get on." He looked across at us. "See you out there when you're ready. Plenty of jobs to do. Ever collected eggs, Alice?"

I shook my head. We sold eggs sometimes in the shop, but they came neatly packed in boxes. Hens had never seemed to have anything to do with it.

I was wearing my old shorts and a faded blue blouse. My pink dress hung on the clothesline still, moving gently in the hot breeze. The dress seemed free of the marks of peaty bog water. Hunger Moss . . . how I longed to get back there.

But the Farmers definitely had other plans. When we'd helped to clear the table, Mrs. Farmer urged us outdoors and we walked slowly toward the farmyard. There was a great deal of brushing and swilling going on in the cowshed, but the cows had gone back to the fields. Mr. Farmer appeared at once and gave us a stern talking to, telling us that we were to keep away from the Moss until Henry could come and take us there. He didn't actually make us promise not to go, but he made it clear there'd be trouble if we disobeyed.

"I'll keep the pair of you busy," he said, smiling suddenly, but we didn't smile back. "There'll be endless jobs you can do."

He introduced us to the young, fair cowman who was called Bob, then led us around the farm. I knew that Adam hated every moment. He was no animal lover and even baby pigs left him cold. I liked the chickens and young animals and was surprised that the calves had so much strength. They had to be fed from buckets; Mr. Farmer explained that they were taken away from their mothers soon after birth.

60

"I expect you've seen kittens born?" he asked, and looked surprised when we shook our heads. We had never had a cat.

"Well, you'll see something born here," he said. And I felt a little thrill of astonishment. I knew about birth, more or less, but it would be interesting and perhaps rather frightening to see it happen. Well, Mother had sent us there to learn. In those old-fashioned times more than twenty years ago, had she seen animals born? Such a thing was never mentioned at home.

The hens were mostly out, scratching contentedly, and there were some very tiny yellow chicks. I vaguely knew that they came out of eggs, which seemed a neat and tidy way to be born, unlike the other. I rather liked creeping into the hen houses and groping for eggs in the warm, smelly straw. Some of the eggs were so newly laid that they were almost hot. They had just come from the hens' bodies. It seemed very clever of them, just as it seemed clever of trees to produce apples and pears. Plums, too. Even the raspberries growing in the kitchen garden surprised me.

When we went in for milk and biscuits, Mrs. Farmer suggested that we should go to the village shop and buy postcards to send to Mother. She told us she'd written to Dad the evening before to say we'd arrived safely.

We grasped at the idea gratefully. Mrs. Farmer offered us money, but Dad had given us five shillings each before we left. To go to the shop gave us a respite from the farm. We had seen Jim briefly, but he had gone into

61

the fields to help the adult workers. We had seen the big reaper and binder surging away to a distant field, where the oats were ripe enough to be cut.

"Call this a shop!" Adam said scornfully, as we reached the cottage that was both post office and store, I thought it was charming, with its festoon of small pink roses. We opened the door and a bell gave a small, tinkling sound. Going first, I fell down two old stone steps and found an elderly woman gazing at me from behind the counter. It must be Mrs. Cox, who had brought the telegram.

"You're Mary Selby's children!" she said instantly. "I remember your mother.... Why, she was just like you," she said to me. "Long hair, and a long dress, but you're the spitting image of her. I've kept this place for forty years. How time passes! Soon I'm going to retire and live with my son in West Guelder."

The tiny shop seemed to have a million things in it, piled up all higgledy-piggledy, and there were delicious smells.

"Did Mother buy things here?" I asked.

"Yes, she always spent her pennies here. Nowhere else to spend them. She liked sherbert suckers and those huge sweets called gob-stoppers."

After more than twenty years, she remembered. But probably few people came to South Guelder from the outside world.

Adam fell for some bull's eyes in a wonderful old bottle, and I looked at the rather old and faded postcards. There were two views of South Guelder, and actually—*actually!*—one of the ruined castle in the middle of Hunger Moss. I bought the two of the village for us to send to Mother, and the Hunger Moss one for myself.

"You can write your cards here," Mrs. Cox said. "There's a pen by the post office counter."

We wrote the cards and stamped them, and poked them into the letter box. Then we sat on a low wall by the churchyard gate and looked at my card of the Moss. It was very dim and brown, but the castle looked quite large. "Some photographer chap took these pictures a long time ago," Mrs. Cox had said.

"It's probably fallen down a lot since then," I remarked wistfully, and Adam grumbled, "I do think Mr. Farmer is rotten!"

"Henry may come soon." How violently I hoped that he would.

All this took us so long that dinner was almost ready when we went back to the farm. After the meal, Mrs. Farmer said there was an afternoon bus into Oxford on Thursdays, and she hurried off to the crossroads to catch it. She wanted to buy a hat for a wedding. The eldest daughter at East Marshlands Farm was soon to be married. Before she left she told us to go "up the fields" and join the others.

Rebellious, but obedient, we started "up the fields." Far away, beyond two fields, we could see the reaper and binder moving up and down, but in the second field was the Guelder Rose herd, peacefully grazing. Peacefully . . . I wasn't at all keen on braving those animals. When we came to that field, Adam stopped abruptly.

I started to open the gate. We hadn't yet discovered if there was a bull with the herd, but even cows had horns and might. . . . "Don't let's," I said.

We turned and went back across the first field and through the gate past the farm buildings. "I wish we could go home," Adam said, so suddenly and sharply that I was startled. "If we went to Hunger Moss again maybe the Farmers wouldn't keep us."

"But we couldn't do that," I said. I was probably as homesick as Adam, and I did find something about the country oppressive, but I loved it and wanted to stay. "There's no one at home, and Dad would half kill us, and what would the neighbors say if we were sent back in disgrace?"

Adam knew something about what the neighbors would say and shrugged gloomily. We turned into the sleepy village.

"Let's look at the church," I suggested, gazing at the ancient building. It stood in a churchyard full of roses. The grass was high around some of the old graves, but near the path it was smooth and patterned with daisies. The air was rich with the fragrance of grass, roses, and honeysuckle.

"It's probably private," Adam said, as I pushed open the lych gate.

64

"I don't think churches ever are," I answered.

Cautiously, rather fearfully, I pushed open the west door. It was immensely thick and old, with a strange dogtooth pattern in the stone above. I had expected darkness and gloom, but the little church was full of summer light. Most of the windows were of plain glass, and we could see trees and the sky. I shut the door gently behind us and we crept down the aisle past the ancient pews. In a side chapel there was a huge tomb, and I was struck by its beauty.

Softly my fingers moved over the stone effigies reclining on top of the tomb. Behind the figure of the man was a row of carved boys, grading down in size to one that was almost a baby. Behind the woman there was a line of girls, all wearing stiff stone ruffs. The lettering on the tomb said: "Robert Guelder and his beloved wife, Caroline. Here they lie with nine of their ten children."

"Oh, come on!" Adam urged impatiently, but still I lingered.

The tomb was Tudor and, I learned later, the one great treasure of South Guelder. The Guelder family had died out in the nineteenth century, and only a pattern on the grass in a field near the crossroads showed where their great house had once stood.

While I was dreaming, Adam had wandered away. I found him by the door that led to the tower. It was unlocked and opened creakily to reveal a spiral staircase.

"Let's go up," Adam said. He began to climb rapidly and I followed, feeling rather scared. It was very eerie, especially when we came to the bells. But it was possible to go on, and Adam continued to lead the way. We came at last to a trapdoor that opened easily. With a shout of triumph, Adam climbed out onto the roof.

It wasn't dangerous. There was a low wall with battlements, but the blaze of hot light was bewildering. We crouched there, looking down on the village; then, turning, we found we could see the whole of Hunger Moss. The far side of the moor was a little hazy but the castle, though nearly a mile away, was clear enough. I longed to be there, searching for the hidden place.

"Oh, I wonder when Henry'll come!" I cried. I leaned on the parapet, staring at Hunger Moss. "You know, Adam, Mother does seem so real to me. I can *see* her going along that old path."

"You talk a lot of rot, Allie. She's always real."

"But just as a *mother* until lately. Did you ever really think of her as a little girl, even when she was telling us the stories? They were just stories. Now they're real and so is she."

"I s'pose so," Adam admitted reluctantly. "I want to go there, anyway."

I'd never thought he had much imagination, but maybe it was stirred by that ancient stretch of countryside. Secret meetings, a secret hiding place, a boy who went away. Just stories, until now.

Adam turned to look the other way and gave a yelp

of surprise. "The cows are coming up! Can't be milking time yet, can it?" We now knew there was milking twice a day.

The whole big herd was slowly approaching the farm, straggled out in a long line. But the farmyard gate was shut, and they wandered past it through the other gate and began to spread out into the village street. Up the fields, the reaper and binder was still working, leaving only golden stubble, and several busy figures were following it, setting up the sheaves.

I glanced at the herd without much interest, then turned to look at Hunger Moss again. It was my turn to cry out because a figure, made very tiny by distance, was leaving the ruined castle and walking rapidly toward the Roman track. It looked like a boy. Once or twice he gave a big jump, evidently over boggy places. Then, reaching the track proper, he turned north and went quickly into the golden haze that was thickening over North Guelder.

"It was a boy!" I whispered, awed and startled.

"Could have been a girl in shorts," Adam suggested.

"He looked like a boy. The way he moved, you know. Reuben's ghost, perhaps." I said it half laughing, half in earnest.

"*Don't* be silly! Just a boy from North Guelder."

"But everyone says people don't go . . . "

Down below there were shouts and a woman in an apron was waving her arms at the Guelder Rose herd. From up the fields came more shouts, and two figures were running. All of a sudden I realized what we had done and dragged Adam down out of sight under the parapet.

We had committed a cardinal sin! Life in the country certainly had its complications.

5 A Castle and a Map

"It's our fault that the cows are in the village," I explained, in great distress. "I did open the gate a little when we were looking at the cows and wondering whether to go. I mustn't have closed it properly, or the other gate either. And you know Mr. Farmer said we must always shut gates. He'll be furious!"

"Oh, heck!" Adam looked hot and cross. "Don't let's hurry back."

We went very slowly down the spiral stairs and carefully shut the tower door behind us. We sat in silence in the back pew, feeling that the church was the only place where we could remain hidden. But the Vicar came in and found us. He was very old, with a worn, kind face, and he seemed to know at once who we were.

"Mary's children!" he said, coming forward, and we stumbled to our feet and shook hands awkwardly. "Adam and Alice Baker, Mrs. Farmer said. How do you do, my dears? My name is Cressington. I've been Vicar here for more than forty years. A very small flock, but nowadays I take services in East Marshland, too. I hope you like my church. You won't have anything so old, mainly Norman, in Liverpool."

69

"I think it's beautiful," I said sincerely, but I was embarrassed in case he asked if we went to church. Dad and Mother never did, and we had only gone to Sunday School sometimes when we were little.

Adam said in his most truculent voice, "We've done something awful. Allie says we left the gates open and the cows are all out in the village."

"Oh, dear!" The Vicar looked closely at us. "Not intentionally, I'm sure. City children aren't used to the importance of gates. You'd better go and face the music, hadn't you? They're in now."

We said goodbye and left the church, but still we lingered. When we returned to the farm, Jim and Bob were doing the milking and Mr. Farmer was in the kitchen, just pouring boiling water into the teapot. Mrs. Farmer had left the meal ready, covered with a big cloth. Mr. Farmer's face was redder than usual and his rage was alarming.

"Told you, didn't I?" he demanded, as we stood shrinking in the kitchen doorway. "Of course I knew it couldn't have been anyone else. Always shut gates . . . *always.* The whole herd out in the village. Wasting time for us, and Sally, great beast she is, broke the glass in the public telephone. Cut herself, too. May have to call the vet."

"We're very, very sorry, Mr. Farmer," I said. "We started to go up the fields to you; then we . . . we decided not to. We didn't go to Hunger Moss. We went to—"

70

"Yes, honest, we're terribly sorry," Adam chipped in, and I knew he didn't want any questions as to *why* we hadn't gone to the harvest field. "We won't forget again."

"Well, of course you come from a city." Mr. Farmer began to calm down. "You've got to learn country ways. That herd's valuable, and Mrs. Barlow's furious because her front garden was trampled over. She takes such a pride in it. Well, get your teas. We decided to milk early. I suppose you can wash the dishes, Alice?"

"Of course," I said, glad that there was something we could do easily.

When Mrs. Farmer came home, with a lacy little hat in a smart green box, she was kinder than her husband.

"It couldn't be helped, but don't forget again," she said. "And, I tell you what, you go and help Mrs. Barlow to tidy her garden. Jim'll be late home, and so will her husband. They'll stay up the fields late every evening while this weather lasts."

"I thought Dad worked hard," I said to Adam, as we walked rather reluctantly out into the village street. "But it's nothing to the way people work in the country. They've all been up since five-thirty."

There were women in most of the cottage gardens, and a small group of children played on a patch of grass past the church. We turned our eyes away guiltily from the broken glass in the public telephone and tried to ignore the many glances cast at us as we passed. Most of them were anything but friendly, and the village certainly didn't look as pretty and tidy as it had done before the cows got out.

Several of the cottages had no fences, and borders and small lawns had been trampled. But none so badly as the garden of Moss Cottage where the Barlows lived. Mrs. Barlow, with a rake, a hoe, and a wheelbarrow, looked both hot and cross, and she didn't seem to have got very far with improving the damage. Broken marigolds, big daisies, and scabiosa lay everywhere, and the soil bore deep hoof marks where the herd had passed.

"Mrs. Farmer sent us to help you," I said, blushing and uneasy. "We're terribly sorry, honestly."

"Well, you may be!" she snapped and launched into a tirade that seemed to last a very long time. Boys and girls from a city didn't seem to rate very highly in anyone's estimation. Adam scuffed his sandals in the dust and looked bored rather than apologetic, and I wished she'd stop and let us get on with the job.

"Truly we're sorry," I said, daring to interrupt. "And your cottage is so pretty, Mrs. Barlow." It was, with clematis and roses growing up the golden stone, neat lace curtains, and a shining brass knocker on the green-painted door.

"Pretty!" she echoed scornfully. "Maybe it is this time of year, but it's a different story in winter. The roof leaks, and there's only cold water, and no sanitation. How'd *you* like to go down the garden path on a winter night to a shed with an orange box over a hole?"

Very much taken aback by this reply to my innocent

remark, I opened my mouth to say that some of the houses in Green Street had no sanitation indoors, but she went on quickly, "The post office is the only cottage with a bathroom, and the Coxes put that in at their own expense ten years ago. Well, if you've come to work, you'd better get on with it." And she gave us short, sharp directions.

After that we all worked in silence for some time. It was sad to see so many broken flowers, but I rather enjoyed the nice smells, the feel of the earth, and the evening sun on my head. I began to think of Hunger Moss and the boy who had been in the tower. If it hadn't been Reuben's ghost, then someone else went there now.

When the garden was tidy again and we had cleared away our tools, Mrs. Barlow's mood softened and she offered us some milk and cake.

"You're not a bad worker when you set your mind to it," she said to Adam. "You're a fine big lad for your age. When you get used to things, I suppose you'll be working alongside our Jim?"

"I s'pose so," Adam muttered, much absorbed in his slice of very good cake, and I rushed in, anxious to hear what she would say. "What we really want is to explore Hunger Moss, but Mrs. Farmer won't let us go until Henry comes and shows us the way."

"The Moss! Oh, you're better away from there. I've never liked the place. It has an atmosphere. Oh, I'm not like some folk. I've been on it, but never all the way over. When I was first married we had a big dog, and he used to take *me* for walks. When I was a child I wouldn't go near it. Oh, yes, I come from these parts; I was born in a village ten miles or so away, and I used to visit my auntie up in North Guelder. She kept the village store in those days."

Mrs. Barlow might have known Reuben. I looked carefully at her. Although her hair was graying and her face worn, she wasn't so very old. Maybe not much older than Mother.

"Did you know Barleylands Farm?" I asked.

"Well, of course I did. It's the biggest farm over there. But the Careys didn't buy much in the store. Stuck up and far better off than most farmers, they were. Gentlemen farmers. Folk say they've softened these days. Did you hear about them from the Farmers? I believe that old feud has died down now. My husband says Roger Carey was at the last big cattle show and he and Bert Farmer talked quite friendly like. But years pass and we people either side of the Moss rarely meet."

"What feud, Mrs. Barlow?" I asked.

"Oh, it was some old trouble over land. Bert Farmer's father, really, not long before he died. The Farmers owned another small farm over the other side of Hunger Moss, and there was an argument over boundaries. Something like that. The Careys were very high handed and there was a lot of bitterness. But Bert Farmer sold the second farm years ago."

74

Suddenly, as if in a dream, I heard Mother's voice: "So that's why we always met at the tower. The Careys would have had a fit if Reuben had come to Guelder Rose Farm. Mrs. Farmer wouldn't have minded, but it was more fun to meet in the middle of Hunger Moss."

"There was a boy called Reuben," I said tentatively. "He stayed at Barleylands Farm every summer when Mother was young. They were friends. Did you know him?"

Mrs. Barlow frowned. "There *was* a boy; a grandson, I think. Red hair and freckles . . . that's all I remember. I only saw him once or twice. I didn't often go to my auntie's."

On the way back to the farm I said to Adam, "You see? That's why they met in the tower, and . . . and that's why Mother never heard any more about Reuben. She couldn't go over to Barleylands and *ask* because of the feud. So she just waited and waited until someone told her. But I think it was awful of him never to let her know. Never to say goodbye."

Another piece of the jigsaw had dropped into place. And there were people at Barleylands Farm now—real people, who had been there then. If they were Reuben Carey's grandparents, they must be pretty old now.

And, oddly, there was now another girl to add to the growing picture. A girl who had been in North Guelder sometimes then, and who had seen Reuben with her own eyes. She hadn't told us her first name, but she'd been wearing a silver brooch, with a delicately wrought pattern, and in the middle of the pattern had been the word "Lily."

Jim met us at the farm gate. He was suntanned and looked tired, and there was straw in his hair. He had done a long day's work, though he was only a few months older than Adam, we had learned.

"Who left the gates open?" Jim taunted.

Adam eyed him with dislike. "Get off!" he said savagely. "It was an accident."

"Some accident!" Jim retorted, grinning. "But then who'd expect anything from town kids? Don't know anything. Cities are nothing but traffic and smells and rotten slums. I bet Liverpool stinks."

"One day I'll biff you!" Adam cried. "Give you a bloody nose."

I rather wondered why Adam didn't go for Jim there and then. At home Adam was never averse to fighting and often came home with his own nose bloody. But at Guelder Rose he seemed curiously diminished; not a bit like his usual self. It must be the strangeness and that awful, secret fear of cows.

It was true that Liverpool had very smelly slums and sometimes, when one was riding on a tram car, the people really stank. Mother sometimes said, "Soap and water costs nothing." But in places there wasn't so much water, and soap did cost something. It was all very well for Jim to be so scornful, but I wondered, with a flash of insight, if the country wasn't, after all, a rather charming slum. Those delightful-looking cottages in

76

the village street, for instance. The country wasn't quite the wonderful dream place it seemed in the summer heat.

But if there was going to be an argument between city and country, then I had to stick up for city. "Liverpool has a museum and art gallery and heaps of theatres," I told Jim. "And big schools . . . all kinds of wonderful things you know nothing about."

"And Oxford has all those colleges. It don't count," Jim said, passing us. "We've got to get the harvest in."

"We won't leave the gates open again," I called after him.

"Better not," he retorted.

Four days passed; four burning summer days when no one seemed to think of much else but harvesting the oats and barley. The wheat, we learned, wasn't ripe yet, but the fine weather would help. On Friday and Saturday, Adam and I helped in the fields, setting up the sheaves into stooks. It was hard and prickly work, but I rather liked it, once I had got the hang of how to make the stooks stand upright. Adam spent some of the time reading a comic in the shade of a hedge and kept away from Jim and Bob all he could. For his secret was out. On Friday afternoon Jim asked him to call up the cows, and Adam, grim and tense, had gone to obey but had retreated with a yell of fear when the herd surged toward him. It caused a lot of mirth, and Adam was ashamed and furious.

We had so much to learn that it wasn't an easy life, but I had taken on the jobs of collecting all the eggs and feeding the hens and calves. I could have been happy, if Adam had been happy, too. A long letter had come from Mother, who seemed to be all right and was looking forward to the convalescent home. There was nothing to worry about on that score.

South Guelder was growing familiar and I knew the names of all the families and much of their history, for Mrs. Farmer loved to gossip when I helped her in the kitchen, or we picked raspberries or gooseberries.

She and I got on very well together, but she could make nothing of Adam, and it wasn't her fault. He wasn't friendly, and I could have kicked him for his attitude.

"You're being rude," I told him, on Sunday morning, when we both sat on the very top of a haystack in one of the big sheds, he reading and I with my diary. My own little diary hadn't enough space for all I wanted to write, so I had bought a thick book at the post office. In it I was putting all I had learned; the names of flowers and a million other things.

"I don't care. They all laugh at me. I hate them!" Adam said morosely.

"Well, it was funny, the way you ran from the cows. They don't understand. Why can't you laugh back?" I asked. He had to get over that fear some time. I almost had already. The cows all had names and were entered in the herd book. They were British Friesians, and, when you really looked at them, their markings in black and white were rather pretty. A new calf was born on Friday night and I was asked to name her. They were all called Guelder Something. So I named her Guelder Grace and drew the pattern of her markings in the herd book. It seemed to help me belong at Guelder Rose Farm.

Adam grunted, and read on. After a minute or two he said, "Why doesn't Henry come?"

"I wish he would. Perhaps he'll come today." It was Sunday and, though everyone had milked and mucked out as usual, no one had gone to the harvest fields.

No one from Guelder Rose had gone to church, either. It was turn about, apparently, and both services were in East Marshland that week. In any case, Mrs. Farmer said she always cooked the biggest meal on a Sunday, and there was certainly a tremendous lot of food in the kitchen. A huge piece of pork was roasting, with roast potatoes, and she was baking furiously.

Hunger Moss brooded, silent and secret, so very near. From the sloping field where we had worked on Saturday we could see it. It was awful not to be able to go there, though it was delightful to lie on top of the crackly hay. I went on writing in my book, casting an occasional glance at Adam. If only he'd read something better than comics he might have passed the scholarship. He had some brains, if he'd only use them.

Teatime came and Henry hadn't arrived; it was a bitter disappointment. As I helped Mrs. Farmer wash the dishes, I tried to get her to talk about Mother and Reuben, but she hadn't a lot to say.

"I never met the boy," she told me, "but I knew Mary met him at the castle. First thing she did every year was to go over there. They both came for their holidays at about the same time. And she'd leave a note, or he would, and they'd meet, and after that there were days when we hardly saw her. I did see their map, but it wasn't finished then. I know nothing about a hidden place. I expect it was just part of a game."

"Oh, there really was one," I said eagerly.

"They used to play they were Romans or something. Then she got big—fourteen—and she wasn't happy that summer. Used to go over Hunger Moss still and come back looking unhappy. In the end she told me. All about how Reuben had come as usual, then, after a few days, never again. So I asked around and found out he had been taken away suddenly by his parents. And the way things happened, Mary never came to stay here again."

"Oh, please let us go out there, Mrs. Farmer," I begged. "It's so hot that Hunger Moss must be dry now. Please!"

"Henry'll be busy with the harvest," she said. "But he'll come. Wait until then."

There seemed no hope he'd come until the next weekend, but Henry arrived on Tuesday, driving a very old car. He was tall and brown faced and very kind and amused.

"Hunger Moss is it?" he said, on being introduced to

us. "Why, Alice, you're your mother over again. I remember how I showed *her*. Come on, then. I can't spare long away from the farm."

We walked eagerly at Henry's side until the way grew too narrow, and he went first over the stile. We followed.

"Tell your mother that we're going to be quite safe here," I urged, and Adam added, "Yes, do! We've waited so long."

"When I've seen how the place is," said Henry. "It's years since I set foot on the Moss."

It was another burning day, with a wonderful blue sky, and the great reaches of the Moss shimmered in the heat. Henry went first, unerringly. Once beyond the bushes we could see ahead, and really it was pretty dry. But here and there were still boggy patches and Henry side-stepped and pointed out how to know where it was safe.

"See that stuff? It's cotton grass. Where that grows it's wet, so don't go. See those stones? Used to be a cottage. I just remember someone living there. She was very old and she died. Strange place to build a house."

We forged ahead so fast that the ruined castle was soon quite near, over to the left away from the Roman track. A faint side path led toward it. Near at hand it looked *very* ruined but was still a definite building, with the tower rising strongly.

"Did you play here?" I asked, breathless with heat and excitement, but Henry shook his head. "I was a farm kid and was expected to work. I had no time for playing after I was nine or so. But I used to come with my dog in the evenings."

We fell silent as we approached the gaping main door of the ruin. It was almost too thrilling a moment. Henry still went first, stepping into a big, gloomy hall under the tower. There was really quite a lot of the castle left ... broken stairs leading nowhere and little dark rooms. It was no longer possible to climb to the top of the tower.

"Strange place!" Henry said. "Men lived here once, guarding the countryside, and the Romans earlier, so they say. Broken steps there ... watch it!"

"Our mother had a secret place here," I said, standing still and staring around. Young Mary and Reuben Carey were there, as attendant ghosts.

"I don't know where," Henry answered, looking very large and everyday. We didn't know, either, but we believed in that secret place. There were plenty of dark passages and black corners. In a space that was less dark because there was a gaping hole in the south wall, we found a wrapper off a chocolate bar that looked fresh and new.

"Someone comes," Adam said, and I remembered the boy we had seen as a miniscule figure, leaving the tower.

"Probably a hiker or one of those naturalists," Henry remarked. "Not many people come, but there are supposed to be unusual birds and flowers on the Moss. Well, if you're careful there's not much to harm you here."

"Can we go right over to North Guelder now?" Adam asked. He looked more cheerful than he had done for ages.

Henry deliberated. "Not much point," he said at last. "I could see that the path looked better on, so you can go another day by yourselves. If it's misty, don't come here. Dad and Mother just weren't sure. They don't know the Moss. Strange that, isn't it, living so close? I'll tell them it's safe for you."

Henry's word was a ticket to freedom, and, strangely, I found the map that very evening. It was in a large atlas on a shelf in my bedroom. The map Mother and Reuben had made so long ago. Too hot to sleep, I had left my bed and crouched down by the books. It was still fairly light, though almost ten o'clock.

There was no doubt about it at all. It was marked firmly at the top "Our map of Hunger Moss," and, in the bottom righthand corner, were the signatures—"Mary Selby. . . . Reuben Carey."

6 The Secret Place and a Stranger

Around the map were little pictures. I didn't think Mother could draw, so maybe Reuben had done those. I turned on the light to see better. There was the ruined castle, with a boy standing on top of the tower . . . South Guelder village, with the church and tiny cottages . . . Guelder Rose Farm and minute cows in a field. At the top of the map was another farmhouse, much bigger and grander, and North Guelder village, with a church with a steeple. On the extreme right was a girl with long dark hair, and on the left a boy playing a whistle.

But my eyes were soon fixed on the castle itself, which was drawn in some detail near the middle of the map. There was a ground plan, showing the big hall, passages and rooms. Close to the extreme west wall in very small print were the words "Our secret place" and an arrow.

I was so excited that I longed to go and tell Adam at once, but knew he was probably asleep. It really seemed like a miracle that I had found the map . . . waiting safely there for Mary Selby's daughter to come and find it so long afterward.

I put it carefully back in the book and presently fell asleep, but long before Mrs. Farmer came to call us I was in Adam's room, displaying my find.

"So there *was* a secret place and I can find it," I said. "Oh, Adam, isn't it exciting?"

Adam nodded, still hot from sleep. "We'll go soon as we've had breakfast."

"We can't do that; not until our jobs are done," I pointed out. "We aren't babies. We can't just rush off. If you help me collect the eggs we'll be all the quicker. That takes ages, for they lay in such unexpected places."

Jim, meeting us in the farmyard as we returned with baskets of eggs, grinned sardonically. "Seen any cows today, Adam?"

Adam glared and said, "You shurrup!" And when Jim had gone he muttered to me, "I've got to get over that thing sometime, but I don't know how."

Mrs. Farmer had packed up a picnic lunch for us; sandwiches, homemade cake, fruit, and lemonade.

"You may as well stay over there," she said. "Henry said it was all right, but do be careful. I don't like the thought of the Moss."

We set off in triumph for the stile. Adam had bought an electric torch at the post office, and I had the map, carefully protected by brown paper. The map even showed where the worst boggy places had been on the Roman track. It was almost as if Mother was with us to act as guide. I wondered what she would say when she saw her map again, rescued from the past. I'd write to her that evening.

We climbed the stile and headed off into Hunger Moss. It had been misty earlier, but by then it was hot and fairly clear. We walked confidently, but looked carefully ahead. We had been at Guelder Rose Farm for a week, and I think we had both changed. The silence of the countryside seemed less menacing.

"I wouldn't mind it here," Adam said, "if it weren't for those cows, and the way Jim and the men jeer at me."

We looked for cotton grass and avoided the places where it grew, and quite quickly the castle drew near. At the point where the sidetrack went off to it, there was a big stone. "The Roman milestone" was printed neatly on the map.

"Was it?" Adam asked.

I stared at the stone, frowning. Once we had had lessons about the Romans in Britain and I had read several books on the subject.

"I think there'd have been letters on it," I said, bending over the great worn stone. "They have them in museums."

The ruined castle looked very eerie and gaunt. I could not take my eyes off it as we approached. Suddenly I gave a cry of surprise and tripped. Adam only just saved me from falling.

"There's a boy on the tower!" I gasped. But, when I looked again, no one was there.

"There couldn't have been," Adam protested. "We saw the stairs and they were broken off. It was dark there, of course, but . . . "

"The boy I saw had red hair!" I was trembling with excitement and a kind of fear. I didn't really believe in ghosts, but it *was* strange country and we were all alone in it. Henry's big figure had been more protection than I'd realized at the time.

"Go on!" Adam said disbelievingly, and laughed.

"Well, you go first, if you're not scared." At the back of my mind I thought, "Reuben's ghost would have whistled a tune."

"Of course I'm not scared. Only of those darn great cows," Adam said bitterly, and he went ahead through the gap of the main door into the shadowy hall. There was no sound.

The steps that led up the tower rose in a corner, shrouded in gloom. Adam shone his light and they were definitely broken off just where they curved out of sight. We went slowly into a dark passageway and looked into each gloomy stone room.

"The secret place was away at the end," I whispered.

I was scared in a way, but determined. My whole life seemed to have led to this, and the girl Mother had been seemed very near. Where she had gone we could go, too. I'd even almost forgotten the boy briefly seen on the tower. He *must* have been in my imagination.

We went on and on and came to the far end of the ruin. The last room was fairly light; there was a gaping space that had been a window. The floor was stony and uneven and the far corner was shadowy. There seemed to be a hole . . .

"Shine a light," I ordered, and at the same moment a voice said loudly, "Hello!"

Startled, I lost my footing and fell into the hole. For a wild moment I thought that I had fallen down a well; then I landed safely, scraping my elbows and one knee. There had been steps, but they were broken, and it wasn't very deep.

Above me Adam was calling, "Allie! Allie, are you hurt?" and a strange voice was saying, "I'm awfully sorry! I didn't mean to startle her."

I rubbed my grazed elbows and stood up. There was still a suggestion of steps and slowly I levered myself up until my head was above ground. My face was close to Adam's. He was crouching on the edge, looking down. Behind him stood a boy with red hair. He wore a white shirt and gray trousers, and had field glasses hanging down over his chest. He didn't look at all ghostly. He had a nice face and brown eyes and he was quite old. Older than I; about fifteen.

"I thought you were killed!" said Adam.

"My fault if she had been," the boy cried, looking concerned.

"I thought you were Reuben's ghost!" I said, still with only my head showing.

"I *am* Reuben," said the boy.

I slipped off my precarious perch and Adam gave a

yelp of dismay. The boy pushed Adam aside and held out a firm, sun-tanned hand to me. "Do come on up! What's the matter, anyway? How did you know my name and why should I be a ghost?"

Hauled up into the stone room, I stared at him.

"You said you were Reuben. It's enough to shock anyone."

"I don't see why. I know it's an old-fashioned kind of name, but it runs in the family."

"She thought you were the ghost of someone else," Adam explained. "We have old-fashioned names, too. I'm Adam Baker and my sister's Alice, though she's often called Allie. We're staying at Guelder Rose Farm."

"I'm Reuben Day and I'm staying in North Guelder. This is the third summer I've come."

"At Barleylands Farm?" I asked, still not sure of reality.

"That's right."

"And you're definitely not a ghost?" But I knew he wasn't. I had liked the warmth of his hand.

"Of course not. I watched you coming over the Moss. I was up on the tower."

"But the steps are broken."

"Well, there's a gap. I got over all right. It's a queer old place, isn't it? I'm interested in bird-watching and in unusual plants, but you don't get much chance in London. I never came over here until this summer. The first year I came I broke my ankle playing football with some younger boys in the village, and last year I went down with measles. What's this about another Reuben?"

We all sat down on the edge of the broken window, where the sunlight fell warmly, and Adam and I started to explain in a kind of chorus. The modern Reuben listened intently and stared at our map.

"Why, that's really strange!" he said at last. "It's jolly rum, in fact. The other Reuben was my uncle; my mother was his older sister. You mean that your mother and he. . . ?"

We went on to tell all we knew. I told the last part, because I had more feeling for the tragedy of it. Mary Selby waiting for Reuben, but he had gone away.

"She waited all alone here," I said. I had thought it sad before, but now it was much more poignant. I wouldn't have cared to be alone there in the middle of Hunger Moss, deserted by a friend. "He never let her know what had happened. His people came and took him away, but he could have sent a message even if there *was* a feud."

"Yes, he could," the second Reuben agreed. His eyes had been almost dreamy while he listened to the end of the story. I thought he was a nice boy, with imagination. "But didn't your mother ever hear what happened to him?"

"No, I don't think she knew, and Mrs. Farmer hasn't said anything, either. Mother said it was as if he had died."

"Well, he did die."

"*Died?* Really?" I almost fell off my stone perch.

"It was before I was born," Reuben said. "I never thought about it much before. It must have been then, soon after he left . . . "

"But . . . how?"

"They were on their way to Scotland; just Reuben and his parents. My mother was going to school at Girton in the autumn and she was visiting school friends, so she didn't go with them. There was a train wreck and they were all three killed. People here *must* have heard about it."

But it seemed clear to me that the Farmers, isolated in South Guelder, had never heard. They had had no contact with the Careys of Barleylands.

"It still doesn't explain why he didn't send a message to Mother before he left," I said slowly.

It was awful that Reuben had died, for he had seemed so real. Maybe his ghost did wander around that lonely place. I wondered what Mother would say when she knew. She had Dad and us, yet . . .

Reuben looked at the map again. "A secret place, you said. Yes, I see . . . must have been somewhere here. Or perhaps it was just a game."

"No," I said. "There was one."

"Well, this is the end wall, so if there is any secret place, it's down that hole of yours, Allie."

We went one after the other down the hole. The space below was cold, dank, and very dark. There was some rubbish, but nothing else. Adam played his light over the stones of the enclosing wall and Reuben gave a cry.

"Look! The stones have been piled up at the end here. There's a kind of opening filled with pieces of rock. Hold the light steady." Quickly he levered a top stone and it came out easily in his hands. A gleam of light shone through. Six stones later there was a gap wide enough to lean through.

Reuben stood back politely while I thrust my head and shoulders in. I was looking into a tiny stone room, with a slit window. There was ivy growing in the gap, but quite a lot of light came through it.

"It's *it!*" I said. "The secret place. But it isn't underground."

"The land drops a little," said Reuben. "I noticed that. If we move two or three more stones we can climb in."

In another two minutes we all stood in the secret place. It was an awesome moment, somehow. It seemed that no one had come since Mary and Reuben had last been there. The remains of their occupation were clearly to be seen. Two cups, two plates, a milk jug, and a teapot with a broken spout stood on a big, flat stone. There was a rusty paraffin stove and an even rustier kettle, and two big, round tins, once with roses painted on them. One had held what might have been tea and sugar, and the other biscuits gone mouldy long ago. They smelled horrible and I shivered.

We stood in silence for quite a time. Even Adam seemed awed, and for me the remote place had a terrifying fascination. Nothing in my life, not even in Mother's stories, had really prepared me for such a spot, miles from traffic and other people.

It wasn't a cheerful place; it was cold and dim and full of the past. But maybe we could make it happy again.

I tried to say what I was feeling, then added, "But we could use it again and it would be better. We could keep our own things here. Mrs. Farmer would give us a kettle, and tea and milk and sugar. I wonder if they carried water?"

"There's a spring outside, behind the castle," said Reuben. "It'd be safe if we boiled the water. There's a little old stove at Barleylands. I saw it one day."

"And it would be our secret," I said, looking at Reuben. "You wouldn't bring anyone else here?"

"No one to bring," Reuben answered. "There are only six boys and two girls in North Guelder, and all much younger than I am."

I wandered slowly around the little room. In an alcove in the wall near the window I found another rusty tin box. The lid had corroded, but I got it open at last. Inside was a piece of paper with thickly penciled writing on it. I saw at once that it was a short letter.

"Dear Reuben," was written in a round, neat hand, "I am leaving this note here in case you come back. I shan't wait here again. I have waited days and days. It was *mean* not to come or let me know why you couldn't. You could have posted me a letter. I thought we were friends, but I feel I'll never forgive you. It's been *awful* all alone here. Yesterday I walked nearly all the way to North Guelder and I almost went to Barleylands. Perhaps you are there and don't want to come." It was signed, "Mary Selby."

I handed the note to Adam and he read it quickly. "*Mother* wrote this?" he asked incredulously. "When she wasn't much older than you? I don't believe it."

"It's true," I said sadly, as Adam passed the note to Reuben. "After she wrote that she learned that he *had* gone away. Perhaps she never has forgiven him for not letting her know."

"Oh, rot!" Adam cried. "All that time ago. People can't remember . . . not grown up people. Not mothers."

"She remembers. You know she does." I put the note in my pocket when Reuben handed it back to me. "I'm not sure I forgive your Uncle Reuben," I said to his namesake.

"Oh, let's get out of here and have our picnic," Adam said, suddenly impatient. So we climbed out and carefully put back the stones. We had hidden our food in a corner, and offered to share with Reuben, but he said he had a picnic, too, and had left it behind a big stone in the hall.

We went outside into the glorious warm sunlight and the Moss shimmered all around. We settled ourselves in a comfortable hollow near the spring Reuben had spoken about, and for the first time really looked at each other in the full light of day. So much had happened within the castle that we had had no time to be shy, but suddenly a constrained silence fell.

I looked at Adam and the animation he had assumed indoors had quite gone. He looked more the way he had been most of the time at South Guelder. He was busying himself unpacking our food and opening the lemonade, but at the same time he was taking covert looks at Reuben.

Reuben was unpacking his food, too, and it was very plentiful, even better than ours. His hair was very bright red and he had a thin clever face. Suddenly I didn't know what to say next. He was quite old, and he came from Barleylands; he also was a Londoner, and Londoners were always said to feel themselves superior beings.

What would he say when he knew that our father was a greengrocer and that we lived in a small house in Green Street? Everything about him suggested money. His clothes, though they weren't new, made Adam's look like rags, and the field glasses looked very expensive. A privileged boy, when I saw him in the open air; I might have known, I thought ruefully, by his voice, but I had been too excited and moved to notice at the time.

It had seemed quite possible for us to be friends while we were making plans in the secret room but now I had doubts, and I had the feeling that Adam's thoughts were the same as mine.

But the doubts, it seemed, were all on our side. Reuben settled himself, with his food arranged on a stone, took a huge bite of ham-and-egg pie, and said cheerfully, "Well, this is good, isn't it? I can't tell you how nice it is to meet you. It's lonely at Barleylands with no one young in the house, and the North Guelder kids aren't much company." And, between bites, he went on to tell us about himself; how his father worked at the Foreign Office and his mother was always busy on committees. He lived in Chelsea and went to a big day school. When he mentioned the name of the school even I had heard of it, little as I really knew about London.

"We were going to Paris, but the way things are the parents couldn't take a holiday, so they said I might as well come to Barleylands."

"How do you mean?" I asked uneasily.

"Well, when there's going to be a war, Father's busy, and Mother said she couldn't be away."

In the warm hollow, in the middle of Hunger Moss, the words rang out with such assurance that I was jerked out of any other thought.

"Do you think there really is?"

Reuben rummaged among paper bags and brought out a large piece of cake. "Of course there is. Everyone knows, except perhaps people who never listen to the news and who are only concerned with *cows.*"

"But . . . how soon?" Adam had been eating stolidly, listening.

"Pretty soon, I suppose."

Suddenly I wasn't hungry any more, and Adam choked on a crumb of cake. When he could speak he said, "Allie and I had better go home if there's going to be a war."

Reuben drank some lemonade, wiped his mouth, and said, still cheerfully, "Oh, there's not that much rush. If you've finished, let's get going. Come on over and see North Guelder."

We rose, packed up all the rubbish, and hid it deep in bracken behind a big stone. It was Reuben who did this, because Adam and I would have left it there, I'm ashamed to say. I know now that it's an awful thing to leave litter in beautiful places. Or in any place at all.

We walked slowly northward over the Moss, with Reuben stopping often to point out a bird or a plant. When we could see the village growing very close, Reuben said, "I'm thirsty again, aren't you? Let's go home and Emily will give us something to drink. She makes the most delicious lemonade."

Adam and I stopped and stared at him.

"To Barleylands?" I asked.

"Yes, why not?"

To Barleylands . . . where Mother had never been able to go. Yet, twenty years after she had gone away from Hunger Moss, we received that casual invitation.

7 We Go to Barleylands

For a few moments it seemed quite possible to accept, but then the feeling came back that Barleylands was forbidden ground. I said slowly, "I don't think we can, Reuben. There was a feud . . . we told you."

Reuben laughed. "Oh, rot! That's over now. You said yourself that Mr. Farmer talked to Great-grandfather at a Cattle Show."

We both looked at him, startled.

"*Great?*" Adam asked.

"Well, they are. My great-grandparents. My grandfather, the other Reuben's father and their son, is dead. Great-grandfather is nearly eighty, but you'd never know. He's so upright and he still gets up at six o'clock to supervise the farm. Oh, come on!" he urged impatiently. "The past's dead, too. How could they mind that you're staying with the Farmers?"

We gave in, but I wasn't at all sure that the past was dead. It seemed very real to me, with that note from my mother in my pocket. We crossed the last stretch of the Moss. Even after the heat wave there had been one or two boggy places, though the path was much better north of the castle. Just in front of the stile there was a stream with a very rough plank bridge. Reuben went first and I looked ahead to North Guelder. It seemed rather larger than South Guelder, with quite a number of golden stone cottages. To the left was the church and, near it, a large farm. I could see a big house, farm buildings, and three huge haysheds. Barleylands!

In another couple of minutes we were in the village. The cottages were grouped around a green and a duck pond, and the little store and post office was next to the inn, which bore a sign: THE CAREY ARMS.

I thought of the girl called Lily, who had stayed here with her aunt and who had seen the other Reuben.

"The front gate's near the church," Reuben explained. "But we'll go in through the yard." And he led the way down a side lane that ended in a white gate. Beyond was a cobblestoned yard and a great many farm buildings. Through a gap between two barns I could see the house. It was built of the local stone and looked huge, more like a manor than a farmhouse.

"I don't think we'd better go," Adam said.

"No, I don't think we had," I agreed.

Reuben opened the gate and motioned to us imperiously. "Well, if you aren't thirsty, I am. And you needn't worry . . . the cows are up the fields."

Something in his tone made Adam look at him. "Don't you *like* cows?"

"I'm scared stiff of them," Reuben confessed cheerfully. "I wouldn't go among them for the world. Great-grandfather's ashamed of me, and all the men laugh. But what do they expect? I'm a Londoner, not a country bumpkin. You're from a city, too. Aren't *you* scared?"

"Yes," I said, looking with joy at the tall boy of fifteen who so merrily said he was afraid. "It's been ruining Adam's life, for everyone laughs at him. They say he's a coward."

"And I s'pose I am," Adam remarked, but there was a different look on his face, as if he had been released from a deep trouble.

"Well, who cares. I'd sooner face a herd of elephants than our great herd when it comes up for milking. Just laugh back and they'll soon find something else to amuse them. In time you may get used to them. I believe you're tougher than I," and he grinned at Adam, who grinned back rather shyly.

"He's as tough as they come in Liverpool," I said. "But the country is so different, and we've only been here a week."

Reuben led the way between the barns into another yard, more a kind of courtyard. A man was washing down a big car, but took no notice of us. The old house loomed above us, the mullioned windows catching the light. In a far corner was an open door and we went that way.

"Another rum thing about the country is that people hardly ever use front doors," Reuben remarked. "Have you noticed that? Even here we don't, unless Great-grandmother has visitors. This way," and he walked through a huge old scullery into an even larger kitchen.

It seemed even older than the one at Guelder Rose, yet there were more modern fixtures. Shyly, as we hesitated in the doorway, I cast a quick glance around. An old woman was making pastry on a vast old table; she was tall, with white hair in a neat bun, and for a moment I thought she must be Reuben's great-grandmother. But Reuben said, "I've brought some friends, Emily. Our throats are as dry as ditches in a heat wave. I'm sure you have oceans of lemonade."

"You'll drown in it one day, Master Reuben," she said, wiping her hands. She opened the door of a pantry and brought out a large blue jug that had a little muslin cap over it. While we drank from heavy old tumblers, Reuben introduced us.

"These are Adam and Alice Baker, Emily. They're from Liverpool, but they're staying at Guelder Rose Farm over the Moss. Emily's been here forever," he added, turning to us. "She must have known Uncle Reuben."

Emily had gone back to her pastry. She said, "Of course I did, Master Reuben, but you never showed any interest in him before. You're as like him as maybe, but you haven't so many freckles."

"Thanks be!" said Reuben. "Their mother knew him. They used to meet at the castle in the Moss."

"He was always over that nasty place," Emily said, but she didn't sound very interested. "Dangerous, I used to tell him, but he just laughed. And you oughtn't to go there, either, Master Reuben."

102

We had finished the lemonade, and Reuben, ignoring the last remark, asked, "Where's Great-grandmama, Emily?"

"In the drawing room, Master Reuben, straining her eyes with her embroidery."

"We'll go and see her," Reuben said, putting down his glass, and he motioned to us to follow him. Out in a dim stone passageway both Adam and I stopped. I said, "Look, I don't think you'd better . . . "

"Oh, you must meet her, if we're going to be friends. We don't want any more rot about not coming to Barleylands."

There seemed nothing to do but to follow him, though I felt shy and uneasy. It didn't seem our world. *"Master* Reuben" . . . how strange!

It seemed quite a long way to the main part of the house but we came out in a large, dim hall that smelled sweetly of roses. Reuben swung to the left and opened a door.

"Great-grandmama! I've brought some friends. At least, I hope they're going to be."

It was a beautiful room, a real drawing room, the kind I had read about in books but never seen before. There were roses in bowls on polished tables, glass-fronted cabinets and comfortable chairs scattered here and there on the rich, dark-red carpet.

It was a big room, too, and we had to walk quite a distance, which gave me time to look around and also to become painfully conscious of my dusty, broken sandals and the fact that I was far too untidy and hot to be presented to the woman sitting at the far end, by the wide-open windows. She made a curiously elegant picture as she sat there in a low chair, her head bent over her work while rainbow-colored embroidery silks lay over a stool at her side. Her white hair was wavy and she was dressed in dark blue. She didn't look a bit like a farmer's wife.

She didn't look up until we stood beside her. She wasn't wearing glasses and her eyes were blue and clear. No sign of the eyestrain Emily had mentioned.

"Well, Reuben!" she said. "New friends? How do you do, my dears?"

"They are Adam and Alice Baker from Liverpool," Reuben explained. "I met them over at the ruined castle on Hunger Moss. They're staying with the Farmers at Guelder Rose Farm."

"That must be nice for you," Mrs. Carey said, in a brisk, clipped voice. Her face hadn't changed at all.

"Yes, it is. Mrs. Farmer is being very kind," I said shyly, but relieved that there had been no reaction. In those first moments I think I became fascinated with Mrs. Carey. She was probably the oldest person I had ever met, but she was still good looking. I wanted her to like me.

Reuben went on to explain. "Their mother used to stay at Guelder Rose when she was a child and she knew Uncle Reuben. She told them stories about the Moss, and never knew Uncle Reuben was dead. Wasn't it awful? She came for years, and she used to meet Uncle Reuben every day out on the Moss, but when he went away that last time he didn't let her know. And so she waited and waited . . . "

There was a change then in Mrs. Carey's controlled face. It was almost imperceptible, but I saw it because I was watching her so anxiously. There was a change in her voice, too, when she said, "He used to meet a Mary Selby. Was that your mother?"

"Yes, Mrs. Carey," I said.

"Where is she now?"

"In . . . in Liverpool. She had an operation on her foot and . . . "

"And so you're getting to know the Moss, too? It isn't a safe place and I don't like Reuben's going there, but he won't listen to me. City children . . . you can't know much about the country. I wonder the Farmers allow you to go to Hunger Moss."

"They wouldn't until Henry Farmer came to show us the way," Adam said. I wondered if Reuben had noticed the change of atmosphere. "And then he said it was perfectly safe if we were careful."

"People have got into trouble on Hunger Moss. I advise you to stay away from it, and you, too, Reuben."

I had the feeling then that Reuben had certainly noticed the slight change in his great-grandmother's manner, but he answered easily, "It's fine, Great-grandmama. You're just being nervous. I think we'll often meet at the castle. It's a good halfway point, and I'm going to teach them about flowers and birds. Not that I know much myself."

She bent to her embroidery again, dismissing us. "You are exactly like your uncle. He would never listen to advice, either."

"May I have that old stove I saw in one of the outhouses and some paraffin for it? We'll keep it over at the castle."

"I suppose so . . . yes. If you insist on going your own way. You're not a child now, and I assume you have some sense. Goodbye, Alice. Goodbye, Adam."

We muttered goodbyes, and Reuben led the way out of the room. We followed him thankfully. Adam pulled a face at me as we reached the door.

We didn't speak until Reuben had led us across the hall, into a short passage, and opened a side door. Then I said, "Oh, Reuben, I think she's marvellous. She's almost beautiful, and she's like a kind of queen. How old is she?"

"Seventy-seven."

"She didn't mind about the Farmers, but when you said all that about Mother, she changed. I think she hated us."

"Oh, what rot!" Reuben cried, but he didn't sound very sure of himself.

"She didn't think we were good enough," Adam said.

"No, it wasn't that." I was glad to be outdoors, though the heat seemed greater than ever. "It was only when you mentioned Mother, Reuben. She remembered her name. And why should she, twenty years later?"

"I don't know," Reuben admitted. "It was a bit odd. I suppose she remembered because there was a feud at that time and she hated Uncle Reuben's meeting a girl from Guelder Rose. Though Great-grandmother isn't a foolish woman, and that does seem rather silly. Most of the time they were only children."

He led us around the house and down the front drive to the gate. The church and Vicarage were near and the cottages dreamed in the sunlight of late afternoon. He was just saying, "I'll see you to the beginning of the path . . . " when a blue car entered the village and slowly encircled the green. A woman was driving, and another woman sat beside her, holding a sheaf of papers.

The car stopped beside us and the woman with the papers got out. She was middle aged and wore a fawn linen suit much the same color as her face. She glanced at us, then over the gate and up the long, well-kept garden to the big house. From that side it looked even more impressive, with its rows of windows and the ancient creeper. In places one could hardly see the golden stone because of the thick growth.

"You, boy!" she cried, looking at Reuben, perhaps because he was the eldest. "Do you live here?"

"Why, yes." Reuben looked surprised. "In the holidays, you know. With my great-grandmother."

"*This* is Barleylands Farm? It doesn't look much like a farmhouse."

"It does from the back," Reuben explained. "Do you want to see someone?"

The driver of the car had got out, too, and was staring around. "Plenty of room here," she said, seeming to be counting the windows of Barleylands. "I should think probably ten. How many people live here?" she asked Reuben.

Reuben said politely, though he looked puzzled, "Well, my great-grandmother and great-grandfather and myself, and two maids and Emily the cook living in. The chauffeur and gardener live in small flats over the old stables."

"I don't suppose you'll keep all those servants if war does come," said the woman with the lists. She sounded rather pleased about it. "Yes, Jean, I should think at least ten and a teacher. But we'll go in and check."

Ten and a teacher! The words really sank in and I gasped. So did Reuben. He jumped to it at the same moment and, in that moment, the dreaming golden peace of North Guelder was shattered.

"She means evacuees!" I cried. I had never really believed it before, that they'd take the children out of the cities and put them in country places. I could hardly believe it then, at least as far as Barleylands was concerned. Our visit to the house had proved that it stood for a peaceful, well-ordered way of life that could never encompass ten strange children. Why, old Mrs. Carey would have a fit! Within herself, anyway. She hadn't seemed the kind of woman to let go openly.

Reuben seemed to feel the same. He said quickly, "I'd better take them to Great-grandmama and soften the blow. Can you find the way back to the Moss? See you at the castle tomorrow about eleven."

We walked through the village almost in silence. Adam picked up a stone and was going to throw it at the ducks but I grabbed his arm and ordered sharply, "Don't!"

Adam dropped the stone and glared at me. His face was very red; part too much sun and part some kind of emotion. He was certainly cross. "But, Allie, do you really think. . . ?"

"Shut up until we're out of the place," I said, for curtains were twitching here and there. With all the strangers in North Guelder, the people were curious.

We climbed the stile, ran over the plank bridge, and faced the two-mile stretch of Hunger Moss. For the moment some of its magic had gone; it just seemed a long way home. Not far along the track there was one of the big stones and I sat down and patted the place beside me.

"Let's sit for a minute and talk. Oh, Adam, what a strange day it's being!" I said. "Sometimes I think that nothing's been quite real since we came to South Guelder. Or else reality has taken over, even though it seems so like a dream."

"Don't know what you're talking about," Adam answered. "Allie, what was all that about evacuees? Mrs. Carey wouldn't have ten city kids within a mile of her,

109

even if there were twenty empty bedrooms. I didn't know people lived like that. At least, I did, but not on a *farm*."

"It isn't an ordinary farm," I said. "I believe the Careys have been there for hundreds of years. Even the pub was called after them."

"She'll send those two women packing with a flea in their ears."

"Perhaps it won't be as easy as that," I said slowly. "Maybe the Government will make a law or something. After all, if there is a war, everything will be different." And I felt my dry throat tighten with fear.

"But, Allie, *is* there going to be a war?" Adam savagely threw a stone into a boggy patch.

"I don't know." But the sight of those two earnest women whose job seemed to be to put city children into safe country homes had gone a long way to convince me that things might be serious.

We had found the remote countryside strange enough, though in a way we had roots there. We had always known about Hunger Moss, and it had been peopled, too. The city children who came might not be a bit like us. I had a vision of the barefoot, screaming children of the Liverpool slums, even of some of the rough boys at Adam's school, and it was *impossible* to imagine them at Barleylands. I thought of the dignity of Emily, the cook, and the way she had said "Master Reuben," and of the polished beauty and cleanliness of the house. Slum children had lice and ringworm, and lived on "jam butties" and fish and chips if they were lucky. How would *they* feel, transplanted into such a lonely place? Would they be enchanted, as I had been, or would they hate every moment away from their real homes?

"But if Mrs. Carey has to take them, so will Mrs. Farmer," said Adam.

I hadn't thought of that. I knew I didn't want anyone else to have *my* room, with its view into the apple tree.

I stood up and stared back at North Guelder and at the many buildings of Barleylands. Over the low hedge that bordered the Moss, I could see the Barleylands herd coming up for milking. It must be getting late. Time for tea. Suddenly I longed to be back at Guelder Rose.

"Let's go!" I said, and we set off across the moor.

8 "Will There Be War?"

Oh, a strange day! Meeting the second Reuben, finding the secret room and Mother's letter, going to Barleylands. I tried to dismiss the thought of war and concentrate on the other things that had happened. The first Reuben was dead, had died soon after his last meeting with Mother, and she didn't know. I shivered in spite of the heat. He had left Barleylands to go to his death in an accident.

"I'll write and tell Mother all we found out," I said after a long silence. We were walking quickly, and the castle was almost even with us. "About Reuben. And about the secret place, of course, and the way we've been to Barleylands. I wonder what she'll think of that? I loved it, in a way. Mrs. Carey was nice at first, but after a bit she did change, don't you think?"

"She's a rotten old snob," said Adam.

"A bit snobbish, perhaps. I don't suppose she can help it. But I don't believe it was that. She didn't seem to mind that we were so grubby and untidy. It was when Reuben talked about Mother and Uncle Reuben that she changed. Didn't you notice?"

Adam nodded. "Yes, I s'pose so, but I think it's because she doesn't like the Moss. No one does."

He might be right and I was making a mystery where none existed. It had all been rather embarrassing; yet I knew I wanted to go back to Barleylands and see Mrs. Carey again. When I said so, Adam laughed with annoying loudness.

"You've a hope, Allie Baker! She may not be able to stop Reuben meeting us at the castle, but she'll tell him not to bring us to her house again."

"Did you like Reuben?" I asked, to blot out the pain of never going to Barleylands again. I wanted it more than the Moss.

"Rather old, isn't he? And a bit posh."

"Posh? Who's being a snob now?" I was all the more angry because of my own first thoughts outside the castle. It wasn't going to have to matter that we were working class and Reuben something different. I didn't think he'd care and I wasn't going to, either.

"Well, I can't talk to a chap like that. Birds . . . flowers . . . a grand London day school. What'll he think when he hears *I* don't go to a grand school?"

"I shouldn't think he'll care a hoot," I said crossly.

"Well, I'd sooner have Jim, if he wouldn't laugh at me."

"I think Reuben's nice, and not a bit like the boys at home." I thought of them gathered on a street corner, eyeing us girls. "I'm going to be friends with him if you aren't."

"Oh, let's get back! I want my tea."

The Moss looked quite different in the glowing late

114

afternoon light, but there was no danger of losing our way. The church tower at South Guelder was a beacon showing through the heat haze. Sticky with warmth and rather dirty, we reached the overgrown stile and tramped tiredly up the lane. The men had evidently worked on in the fields and the Guelder Rose herd was just coming up for milking. The first cows were approaching the cowshed as we turned toward the garden gate. Jim, waving a stick, grinned at us.

"You lazy lot! You should have been doing some work. But Adam's scared of cows."

Adam leaned on the farmyard gate. Suddenly I thought that he looked bigger than he had been. He couldn't have grown fatter and taller in a *week*.

"We've just met a boy of fifteen who says he's terrified of cows and he doesn't mind who knows it."

"Must be a sissy, then!" Jim retorted scornfully.

"He isn't, so you shut up, Jim Barlow! He's a Londoner and he's Mrs. Carey's great-grandson, and if he's scared of cows, I can be, too."

Jim looked taken aback at Adam's aggressive tone. My brother had been quite literally "cowed" since he arrived at Guelder Rose.

"You been over to Barleylands?"

"Yes, and the cook gave us lemonade and we met Mrs. Carey."

"You went across the Moss?"

"That's right."

"Well, if you crossed the Moss that's more than I'd

do," said Jim, and he urged the stragglers into the cowshed. It seemed to me a handsome admission and I began to hope that things would be better between the two boys.

Mr. Farmer had finished his tea and was just going out again. Mrs. Farmer had waited for us. There was the usual delicious meal, but she looked flustered and unhappy.

"I had two visitors," she told us, as she poured out. "Couple of women, nosy as you please. Wanted to know how many spare rooms I have here."

"Oh!" I gasped. "Were they in a blue car, and was one wearing fawn color?"

"Yes. You saw them, too? They came about dinnertime, just as I was expecting Bert back from the fields. This isn't a mansion, I said to them. And I told them, now I've two guests, there was only one bedroom free and the attics, and most of those packed with junk. I can't think what things are coming to, trying to cram Birmingham children into our private homes."

"Mother said you love children," I remarked, and she gave a kind of snort, then laughed.

"Well, there's children and children, and, when it comes down to it, children are people and you like some and not others. And I don't like to be frogmarched into things by interfering women. When there's real danger it may be different, but meanwhile it's harvest time and I've all Bert's shirts and socks to wash. Gets so sweaty, he does. I'm washing every single day."

116

"But they're not going to cram them yet, are they?" Adam asked.

"I'm sure I don't know. They kept on talking about the emergency." Then she looked at us searchingly. "You didn't wash and I won't have dirty hands and faces at my tea table."

We rose and went meekly to wash at the kitchen sink. Occasionally Mrs. Farmer addressed us as if we were very young, but it didn't seem any good arguing. Certainly our hands and faces *needed* washing, and Mr. Farmer wasn't the only one who got sweaty.

"I don't see why all our lives should be upset because of that Hitler," Mrs. Farmer said, as we began on the meal. "But one thing's certain; our Henry is safe. They won't call up farmers, though they may go for the farm workers."

"If there's going to be a war we must go home," Adam said.

"All in good time. It's probably just another scare, like last year. Enjoy your tea. At least you came back safely from the Moss."

We began to tell her about our astonishing day. She listened avidly, drinking cup after cup of tea. "Another Reuben? My! And the one Mary used to know dead these many years? She'll be sorry to hear that. Very taken with him, she was. First love, I always thought it."

"I asked Mother and she said she wasn't in love with him," I told her.

Mrs. Farmer shook her head sagely.

"In the country that sort of thing always started earlier. Why, Bert and me knew we'd be wed when I wasn't so much older than you, Alice. Me fifteen, he sixteen. That last year your mother was getting too old to go meeting a boy alone out there on the Moss, but there was no need to say anything. He went off. And you're telling me you really went to Barleylands and met the old lady?"

We told her the rest of what had happened; most of it. I did more of the talking and I didn't say that she had turned unfriendly—or something—when our mother was mentioned. I still felt that there had been a bit of a mystery concerning Mrs. Carey's changed manner, and I didn't want to tell Mrs. Farmer.

Alone in my room that evening, I read Mother's note again, then tore it up. She wouldn't want that back; it was better to destroy it. Then, kneeling by my window in the last of the daylight, I wrote to Mother, telling her about the happenings of the day. Near the end of my letter I wrote: "If there's going to be a war we'd better come home soon. It would be awful not to be with you and Dad when terrible things are happening. But I do love it here."

When I had sealed up the letter I suddenly had a startling thought. Somehow, even through all the talk of evacuees, I had forgotten that they might try and evacuate *us*. There had been emergency plans to take the girls from my school to North Wales, and Adam's new school would have plans, too.

I didn't *want* to be evacuated to North Wales; I'd

sooner stay in Liverpool and face what came. I wondered what Jenny thought about it and decided to write and ask her. I had sent her a postcard and had one back from her.

I dreamed wildly that night; first troubled dreams about war, and then about the Moss and Barleylands. Mrs. Carey figured largely and, on the moment of waking, I heard her voice saying clearly, "I like you, Alice Baker." But I knew that was just me wishing it.

After breakfast and chores, Mrs. Farmer gave us tea and milk, an old kettle, and a very substantial packed meal, and we set off across the Moss. Adam hadn't seemed very keen to go, and I said, "I thought you longed to go on the Moss. You are an odd boy!"

"I did when we weren't allowed to," Adam answered. "But we've seen it now, haven't we?"

"You mean twice is enough?" I asked, amazed and disgusted. The old moor still drew me powerfully, and my heart lifted with excitement as the castle drew near.

Adam shrugged. "I don't mind climbing to the top of the tower, but there's work to be done at Guelder Rose, isn't there?"

I was so surprised that I didn't answer. Adam wanting to *work!* Probably it was just that he was shy of Reuben, and that was silly. Yet I felt shy myself when I saw Reuben sitting by the main entrance of the castle with the stove and a can of paraffin at his feet.

Reuben greeted us cheerfully, and we hid all our things; then he led us to the top of the tower. Once we'd crossed the broken space it really was quite easy, and the view was new and thrilling.

Reuben lent us his field glasses and we could see quite far away, even though there was a heat haze.

When we came down from the tower he led us over a side path, very boggy, to a little pool and showed us flowers (I entered them in my diary notebook, which I had in my pocket) and the remains of a cottage that wasn't marked on Mother's map. It still seemed strange to think that people actually lived on the Moss in olden days.

Reuben didn't mention Barleylands or his great-grandmother until we had nearly finished our picnic; then he asked casually, "Can you both come to tea tomorrow?"

"To *Barleylands?*" I gasped, for I really had thought we might never go there again. Seeing it through the glasses, I had yearned for it, and wondered what Mrs. Carey was doing on that hot morning.

"Of course to Barleylands," Reuben answered, looking amused. "Where else?"

"But. . . . Did Mrs. Carey say we could come?"

"She's invited you both," Reuben said. "We were quite wrong, it seems, when we thought there was something odd about her manner. She was awfully upset at first about those two women, but she seems sure it'll never come to taking strange kids. I think she's being a bit optimistic there. Anyway, when she calmed down, she said you seemed a nice pair and it was pleasant for me to have companions near my own age. So you'll come, won't you?"

Go to Barleylands again and have tea! Even if we had it in the kitchen with Emily and the maids, it would be marvelous. I didn't think Adam was as pleased by the invitation, but in any case it seemed like a royal command.

When we returned to Guelder Rose, Mrs. Farmer took the same view, and when Adam said he'd sooner not go she threw up her hands. "If the old lady has asked you to tea you *must* go. My, wonders will never cease! I never thought I'd live to see the day!"

Reuben was going out to lunch with his great-grandmother the next day, and we had arranged to meet at the castle at three o'clock. Adam and I worked in the fields in the morning and I noticed a change in Jim's attitude to him; even the men seemed to have accepted Adam, and not one jeering word was said about cows. After our midday dinner, Mrs. Farmer ordered Adam to put on his best shirt and trousers, and me one of my school dresses and my second pair of sandals. Adam grumbled that it was daft to get dressed up to walk across the Moss, and we had to be very careful climbing the overgrown stile, as there were so many brambles.

The good weather was continuing, though it wasn't as hot as the day before, and it seemed quite natural to be heading across the Moss. Already we knew exactly where the bad places were and avoided them.

"Gosh!" Reuben cried, when he saw us. He was sitting on the Roman milestone where the path went off to the castle. "Aren't we grand?" *He* wore his usual clothes, so he had evidently changed after being out with his great-grandmother.

"Mrs. Farmer made us," I explained.

"Well, I do like your dress. It's so neat. You look much older than you did in shorts." And he eyed me so carefully that I felt myself blushing. But his was friendly interest and not a bit like the looks the boys in Liverpool cast at us girls.

We didn't have tea in the kitchen with Emily; we had it in the drawing room, with one of the young maids to wait on us. Mrs. Carey was very gracious, with no sign of strain or unfriendliness, and Mr. Carey came in and joined us. He certainly didn't look nearly eighty; he was a very good-looking man, with crisp white hair, a brown face, and what I thought of as distinguished features. He asked after the Farmers in a perfectly friendly way, and he and Adam talked about farming. That is, Mr. Carey did most of the talking while Adam listened, though my brother asked a few questions and began to look much less shy and awkward.

I could hardly believe that I was actually sitting there in that lovely room, drinking tea from a delicate china cup and eating cucumber sandwiches, hot scones, and tiny little cakes. Being waited on by a *maid*. I was terribly shy at first, but Mrs. Carey asked about my school and what books I liked, and I soon found myself talking quite easily. Mother and Uncle Reuben weren't mentioned, nor was the Moss.

Mrs. Carey did eventually refer to the question of the ten evacuees.

"I suppose," she said, pouring out more tea from the silver teapot, "that if war does come we'll have to manage somehow, but poor Emily nearly had a heart attack when I told her. I'm afraid," and she smiled wryly, "that we're set in our ways, and at my age it isn't easy to change and face the thought of a new way of life. I like peace and quiet above everything." And she looked through the old windows across a smooth lawn to a rose garden. "I don't suppose Mrs. Farmer likes the idea, either. She isn't as young as she was."

"No, she doesn't like the thought," I agreed. "But it's the Vicar's housekeeper who's really upset. The Vicar told us when he came to Guelder Rose after breakfast this morning. The Vicarage is pretty big and those women told him they could probably take five or six children."

"Poor Cressington," she said. "He's soon going to retire, I hear."

"Next spring, he said," I explained. "*He* doesn't seem upset. He was talking about his Christian duty."

Mrs. Carey laughed rather harshly. "He would! He has to, in his calling. I don't like to be reminded of mine, but if war comes we'll have no choice. Children can't be left in Birmingham and London to be bombed."

Mr. Carey rose. "I must go out again; see how they're getting on. My bones tell me it'll rain tomorrow. Oh, don't worry, Miranda. It'll all blow over. Hitler'll think better of it."

Miranda! Oh, it didn't seem real . . . any of it. Mrs. Carey hadn't actually said "I like you, Alice Baker," but she *did* say, as we rose to go a few minutes later, "You must come again. I like young people in moderation. If I'm out, Emily will always give you tea."

"And," murmured Reuben, as we went outdoors, "Emily'll give us a more substantial spread. I can eat those cucumber sandwiches in one bite, can't you? But we have dinner at seven-thirty, and Great-grand-mother has a small appetite."

Reuben walked almost all the way back across the Moss with us, and he and I continued the conversation about books. We liked much the same authors. Adam walked behind us, looking bored. I wondered what Mother and the other Reuben had talked about, as they grew older.

"I do like your great-grandmother," I said, as we were parting not far from the stile on our side of the Moss. "Admire" would have been a better word.

"Oh, she's O.K.," Reuben agreed. "A bit stiff, but Emily says she isn't half as stiff and proud as she used to be. Emily came to Barleylands when the great-grandparents were first married, and that was fifty-five years ago. Well, see you tomorrow. Picnic again? About eleven, if it doesn't rain."

But it did rain. I awoke in the night and heard the drops pattering on the leaves of the apple tree, and in the morning the rain was falling softly and steadily, and everywhere was lost in mist. I had had a wakeful night, thinking of Barleylands and Mrs. Carey, and telling myself how wrong I had been to think there was any mystery.

It was strange to see the country in rain, and in a way rather nice. The air was filled with delicious smells. We did our usual jobs, wearing our raincoats and borrowed rubber boots. Very old boots that were rooted out of a cupboard under the stairs; they had belonged to Henry. The cows were in the fields, as usual, and Jim and Bob were going to whitewash the cowshed. Adam said he'd help. I went out into the kitchen garden to pick what ripe raspberries I could before they spoiled, and, while I worked, I thought of the Moss and Reuben. But Mrs. Farmer would never let me go while it was so wet and misty. It was very frustrating.

9 Uncertainty

The frustration continued. I picked runner beans for dinner and helped Mrs. Farmer in the kitchen, but after the meal I was growing very restless. The rain was still falling softly, and the mist was still thick. It was Saturday, so the men were off until milking time, but Jim and Adam were cleaning harness. They seemed to be getting on all right. Adam was settling down, even though he still avoided the cows.

There had been a letter from Mother that morning, from the Convalescent Home. She was nearly better and could walk quite well. She had had mine about the Moss and Uncle Reuben, but she didn't say much about that, except to tell us to be careful of the Moss. In answer to my remark about war she wrote, "Don't worry, Allie. Your father is sure it will all pass over. Just enjoy yourselves, and rest assured that, if things look worse, we'll be in touch."

So we had a long time yet at Guelder Rose; time to get to know Reuben really well, and to go to the Moss and Barleylands. I knew by then that it would be awful to go away, but I told myself that we could come back, as Mother had done, in other summers.

Thinking thus, I went out into the garden again to cut

off dead flowers, and, hearing a bicycle bell, I looked beyond the gate and saw Reuben.

He said he always brought his bike to Barleylands. I took him into the kitchen, where Mrs. Farmer was making bread, and I could see she liked him at once. It was strange to see *my* Reuben there, where the other Reuben had never set foot.

Mrs. Farmer told me she had an old bicycle she hardly ever used now. It was in one of the sheds. "Just to go over to East Marshland occasionally," she said. "I'm getting too old for cycling. See if the tires are all right, Allie, and you and Reuben go for a ride. You can cycle?"

I told her I had often borrowed a bike, though I didn't own one. It seemed a lovely idea to ride through the soft rain and mist, and we set off cheerfully. We went to West Marshland and looked at the church, which was very tiny and pure Norman, Reuben said. And on around the Moss in a clockwise direction, passing the very small village of West Guelder and so into North Guelder, where we looked at that church, which had a tomb even more interesting than the one in South Guelder. On again into East Guelder, which had no church at all, and then to East Marshland, which I hadn't yet seen. Mrs. Farmer had given me a note to take to the farm, where the daughter's wedding was to take place next Saturday. The farmer's wife, Mrs. Blade, asked us into the vast old kitchen and gave us milk and raspberry pie. She showed us the secret hiding place behind the chimney breast.

Oh, I was learning so much, and loving every moment, especially in Reuben's company. He knew such a lot, though he did come from a city, and if the other Reuben had been half as nice then I fully understood Mother's sorrow when she didn't see him again. The strange thought went through my mind that, if Uncle Reuben hadn't gone away at exactly that time, and gone to Scotland on that particular train, he might have been my father. For maybe Mother *would* have managed to go back to Guelder Rose if things had been different, and maybe first love would have turned into married love.

But I wanted my own father, of course; my dear father, who worked so hard and looked so worried.

Reuben and I parted at the crossroads, near the blacksmith's, planning to meet by the castle on Sunday afternoon, if the rain stopped, and I rode back through the village. How long it seemed since Adam and I let the cows out and stood on top of the church tower. We weren't really alien any more. The villagers seemed to have forgiven us, and in a week and a half we had begun to belong. Oh, dear South Guelder! I thought. Dear Guelder Rose!

The next week passed with incredible swiftness. It became the accepted pattern for Adam to work with

Jim and for me to go and meet Reuben, either in the middle of the Moss or on our bicycles somewhere on the outside. The weather had grown hot again, and the world was drowned in the growth of high summer. I adored it and was learning the names of birds and flowers all the time. I knew where rare orchids grew on the Moss, and where there would be wild iris and marsh marigolds in springtime. I went to Barleylands twice more and began almost to feel at home there, and Reuben came to Guelder Rose for tea.

Toward the end of the week we began to cycle farther afield, and on the Friday we actually went into Oxford. It wasn't really very far, but it was another world; a world of wonderful Colleges, of Magdalen Tower and glowing gardens, of old streets and interesting bookshops. Liverpool and Green Street seemed a thousand miles away, but they were always somewhere at the back of my mind. I heard little news at Guelder Rose, but Reuben brought newspapers for me to see, and the headlines looked frightening.

The dream time would come to an end, but while it lasted it was heavenly, and I was so happy. I *knew* it would end, I had convinced myself at last that war would come, but few people in the villages around the Moss seemed in the least concerned.

Adam and I went with the Farmers to the wedding in East Marshland, and the bride was very pretty and only nineteen years old. The reception was held in the village hall, some of the men got very drunk, there were roses outside, and we threw so much confetti as they drove away for a honeymoon in Brighton that it lay on the ground like snow.

Yet Mrs. Farmer and the Vicar and the Careys had received official notices about evacuees.

"When are you going home?" I asked Reuben, as we stood on top of the castle the following Monday.

"Oh, September some time," he answered. "School doesn't start until the twentieth."

"But you can't stay in London if there's war."

"I could," he said. "They can't *force* people to send their children away. And I'm not a child; I'm too old to be bundled off into safety. Though my school has some kind of evacuation plan."

"Adam's school opens before the end of August," I remarked. "Some Liverpool schools have always gone back very early. Mine's like yours . . . later. Mother hasn't said exactly when we're to go home, but it must be next week, and even then Adam'll be late back. I asked Mrs. Farmer, but she just looked vague. In some ways," I confessed, gazing north toward Barleylands, "I can't *imagine* being back home, in my own room there, and hearing the trams rushing along Smithdown Road."

"This place lays a spell," Reuben said. His face was somber. "This year I've really felt it."

"They say the Moss gets you," I remarked and looked all around at that mysterious place, known by then but no less strange. "I thought it meant the bog gets you,

131

but maybe it's not as simple as that. But we have other lives, don't we?"

"Of course we do," he agreed briskly, but he was looking, too.

"Don't you *want* to come to the Moss and to Barleylands again?" I asked Adam that evening. We were growing apart in some ways.

He shook his head. He had grown taller and was burned brown by the sun. He seemed totally unlike the boy who had been brought home in disgrace by a policeman.

"But Reuben asks about you and so does Mrs. Carey."

"Let 'em ask!" said Adam. "I'll come in my own good time."

So the week passed and still Mrs. Farmer was vague, and Mother's letters told us nothing very much. Just that she was home and well, Dad was busy, and Liverpool was very hot.

I was sure there'd be a letter on Monday saying we must go home, for Friday was September 1 and Adam surely mustn't miss any more school. Not that he seemed worried about it. But there was no letter for us, though the Farmers had several.

"Mrs. Farmer," I said, as I was packing up my picnic food before going to meet Reuben, "it's been heaven here, but it's time we went home. Only . . . you will let us come back another summer, won't you?"

Mrs. Farmer banged the frying pan rather loudly as she washed it, and didn't answer at once. Then she said,

"I'm glad you've both been happy here, Allie."

"Oh, I truly have. I can't bear the thought of leaving, but after all, our home's in Liverpool, and Dad and Mother . . . "

"And you're sure Adam's happy, too?"

"Oh, yes, I think so," I answered earnestly. "I never thought he'd work so hard. Of course he still keeps away from the cows . . . "

"He's a good lad. Bert thinks well of him. All he needed was to get away from that lot he'd grown friendly with in Liverpool."

I stared at her. "You knew about that? That he was nearly in trouble because he'd been silly?"

"Your mother told us, and about failing the scholarship. There are other things besides book learning, though of course you're different. At a grand school and all."

"Adam was just lazy. He isn't stupid."

"Hadn't found the thing he'd like to do. Well, get off, if you're going," she said, almost sharply. "Bring Reuben back to tea, if you like."

Hadn't found the thing he'd like to do! I chewed over her words as I walked across the Moss, but at the back of my mind was the pain of what she *hadn't* said. I would have given anything for a reassurance that we could come back to Guelder Rose. As for Adam, was farming the thing he liked to do? He had certainly learned a lot and was reading *The Farmer's Weekly* instead of comics. But he couldn't farm if he wouldn't go near the milking herd and, in any case, when could he work on a farm again?

Reuben was sitting outside the castle, reading, and he had brought a couple of books for me. When we weren't looking for flowers or observing birds, we often just sat and read. We kept the stove and a few other things in the secret room, but it had remained a sad place and we never spent long in there.

While we waited for the kettle to boil I said, "I can't think why mother hasn't arranged for us to go home. It's beginning to worry me, though I don't *want* to go."

"I feel the same," Reuben admitted. "I think I should go home if there's going to be a war, and there is, you know, Allie. It seems pretty definite now. They have plans to evacuate the children on Friday. Great-grandfather had a notice today. They're going to set up some kind of center in the village hall, and . . . "

I was shocked and startled. "You mean it's as definite as that? Then the Farmers and the Vicar must have had notices, too, and no one said a word. I don't understand it."

"Great-grandmother says I must help until I go away. She's counting on me."

While we were having our picnic outside the castle, I tried to convince myself that city children really would come to that isolated corner of England but couldn't really imagine it. When I returned to South Guelder (alone, because Reuben's great-grandmother had visitors and wanted him there) I went straight into the post office and asked Mrs. Cox for a telegraph form. I had some money, because Mr. Farmer had given us half a crown each on Saturday. I sent the telegram to Dad. "Please let us know when to come home. Worried about war. Allie."

Counting the words with a blunt pencil, Mrs. Cox said, "We're all worried, Allie, but I think it'll pass over in spite of all that's going on. You really want this to go?"

"Yes, please. And, Mrs. Cox, don't tell the Farmers until there's a reply."

But there was no reply by eleven o'clock the next morning, when Reuben came on his bicycle. We had planned to go for a long ride. There seemed no point in hanging around the farm, so I got out Mrs. Farmer's bike and we rode off through the lovely narrow lanes to villages that we hadn't seen so far. And after a while, happy in Reuben's company, and as usual adoring the passing summer scene, I put the thought of going home out of my mind.

Reuben came back to tea and there was no mention of a telegram; nothing said about our going. When he was leaving, Reuben said, "I'm going out with Great-grandmother in the car tomorrow. We're visiting some people near Reading. So let's meet at the castle about eleven on Thursday, Allie."

We were standing by the green-painted gate, I leaning on it from the inside. Behind me the garden was beginning to have suggestions of autumn. Dahlias and

Michaelmas daisies were in bud, and the goldenrod had opened. In the orchard the apples and plums were almost ripe, and my heart was stabbed with sorrow because I wouldn't be there to help pick the fruit. Because there *must* be some news tomorrow. Maybe we'd have to go suddenly, and by Thursday I might be far away.

There was a telephone at Barleylands, and I could phone from the call box by the post office. When I said this, haltingly, to Reuben, his face changed. We looked at each other for a very long moment.

"It might be goodbye," he said, at last.

"It might be," I said sadly. "But I'll leave a message."

And then, without actually saying goodbye, we turned away from each other.

I went slowly into the house, sure that the uncertainty would soon end.

10 Full Circle

The next day, Wednesday, Mrs. Farmer seemed to be planning to cook even more food that she did on Sundays. There was a huge piece of lamb ready to go into the oven, pounds of potatoes being scraped, and plans for gooseberry pies.

"Is it for the evacuees, Mrs. Farmer?" I asked, but she shook her head and told me to go and bring in a really ripe marrow.

In the kitchen garden I chose the marrow and cut it and walked into the front flower garden with it, warm from the sun, in my arms. And then I had the most enormous shock, for a van was approaching the farm, was stopping outside the green gate. It was a familiar van, the one we had last seen at Woodside Station. Miracle of all miracles, Dad was at the wheel, and Mother opened the door and began to climb out. I dropped the marrow and ran.

I flung myself into Mother's arms, almost crying. I just couldn't believe it . . . that she was back at Guelder Rose. She hugged and kissed me, and Dad kissed me, too, and said how well I looked and how I had grown.

"But. . . . But how? But why? Have you come to take us home?"

"We left at five, and the shop is shut for the day," Dad said, looking around and stretching himself in the sun. "So this is your wonderful Guelder Rose, Mary? I must say it's a pretty place. I didn't know England was like this. It's been a revelation to me, these last miles."

Then Mrs. Farmer was there, not looking surprised, and Adam, very surprised, appeared from the farmyard. We went into the kitchen, all talking at once. Mrs. Farmer produced tea for the travelers with incredible speed and, while they drank first cups, insisted on boiling eggs and making toast, as dinner was still hours away.

Mother sat staring around as if *she* couldn't believe she was at Guelder Rose. She was quite tanned, with her hair fixed prettily. She said she had spent a lot of time sitting in the garden of the Convalescent Home and felt better than for years. Dad looked pale and tired, but then he had driven a long way.

"It seems like yesterday that you went away, Mary," Mrs. Farmer said. "In spite of these two large young people."

"There have been a lot of yesterdays since then, but I remember it all," Mother answered. "And when I saw the Moss from the top of the hill . . . "

"Now don't say you want to go onto that nasty place!" Mrs. Farmer protested. "I've never been happy about Allie going over there, though she's come to no harm."

So many dreamlike things had happened since we came to Guelder Rose that, in some ways, it just seemed another unlikely thing that Dad and Mother were *here*. But there must be a reason for their visit, and that reason must be to take us home. Away from the Moss, and Barleylands, and Reuben. But Reuben would be going, too, before very long.

I waited anxiously for something to be said, but nothing was; the talk was quite general. I was growing uneasy and restless when Mother announced, "We'll take a stroll outside and the children can show their father the village." And, quite firmly and quickly, she got us all outdoors.

Adam kicked me and muttered, "What's it all about, Allie?" and I shook my head. But I was sure we were leaving and I began to look at everything more carefully than usual so that I'd never, never forget.

We strolled into the village street and past the post office and came to the churchyard gate. There was a seat in the churchyard in the shade of a yew tree and Mother turned that way. We all sat down and there was rather a long silence. Unable to bear it any longer I burst out, "You've come to take us home, haven't you? But you might have answered my telegram, or let Mrs. Farmer tell us. We aren't babies to be kept in the dark about things."

"No, you aren't babies," Mother agreed. "You both look much older, somehow. But it was better to come and see you, and explain. And it was to be a surprise."

"Explain?"

"Yes." Mother began to speak quickly. "We hope

you'll be happy about it when you get used to the idea. You're staying at Guelder Rose with the Farmers. For a few months, anyway, until we see what happens. No, listen a minute," as Adam started to speak. "You'd be evacuated, in any case, on Friday. It seems the plans are going ahead."

"But we wouldn't have to *go*," I whispered, utterly taken aback. "We could have stayed with you. We *want* to be with you if something awful is going to happen. Haven't we any choice in the matter? I'll be fourteen on Sunday. That's old enough to decide."

Dad started to say, "Rubbish, Allie! You're still—" but Mother gave him a warning look across Adam and said quickly, "In some ways you are old enough, Allie. But we're old-fashioned parents, and we do want what seems best for you. We can't leave Liverpool because of the shop, but you *can* and you should. So you can choose in a way, but the alternative is to be evacuated with your schools on Friday, and Adam's missed the beginning of term."

Stay at Guelder Rose! Be there to pick the fruit and see autumn turning into winter. The thought of winter in the country had a strange fascination. I could sit and read in the inglenook, and see the snow lying over fields and over the Moss, instead of all dirty and slushy in city streets. But . . . not to be with Dad and Mother in the time that was coming!

"What about school?" I asked, remembering that I

had to be educated properly if I were to have a chance at college.

"Oh, that's more or less fixed," Mother told me cheerfully. "Your headmistress knows all about it, Allie. She returned early from her holiday and I saw her at the school on Monday. You can be transferred to a good high school this side of Oxford. Dad's bought you a bicycle for your birthday, so you won't have to borrow Mrs. Farmer's old one."

"And Christmas as well," Dad chipped in. "It's in the van, with all your winter clothes."

"And we brought you this, too." Mother opened her bag and took out a lovely little wrist watch. "I'm sure you need a watch here. And when the weather gets bad, Mrs. Farmer says there's a bus from the crossroads at eight-thirty all school days. Three of the East Marshland boys and girls go to school in Oxford, and a few others from round about. Adam? Oh, he can go to East Marshland School. Mrs. Farmer says the teacher is the best for miles around. She really pushes children, and puts the promising ones in for special scholarships."

"So it's really all arranged?" Adam asked slowly. "We *haven't* any choice."

"Yes, you can still come North with us this evening," Dad said. "But think carefully, you two. Make no mistake, we'll miss you, but now I've seen this place I think you'll be happy here."

"We *are* happy here, but it was only for a holiday."

In the pain of those moments I forgot how anxious I had been for a chance to come back.

But I knew we'd stay at Guelder Rose. If we insisted on going home, Dad would see we were evacuated on Friday, and the thought of being with total strangers was dreadful. "I wish Hitler would drop dead!" I added shakily.

"A lot of people wish that," Dad said grimly.

After that we walked up the village street and back, then started down the narrow lane to the Moss. But Adam said suddenly, "Let Mother and Allie go, Dad. Come and see the farm and meet my friend Jim. I know a lot about farming now and it's jolly interesting. I wouldn't mind being a farmer when I grow up."

"Then you'd have to stop being scared of cows," I said over my shoulder. It was unkind, but I felt. . . . Oh, I didn't know how I felt. Churned up, and mixed up, and I *wanted* to say something nasty.

Adam was silent, and Dad asked, "Is he? I don't blame him."

"I keep away from 'em," Adam muttered. "I do all the rest. Jim and the men laughed at first, but they've got used to it."

Mother and I went on, in silence, to the stile. When I saw the Moss in front of me, secret and quiet in the sun, I felt better, but I was aware that it was a strange moment. Mother back at Hunger Moss . . . Mary Selby, who had waited in vain for the other Reuben.

Mother climbed the stile nimbly. She was walking

pretty well, I had noticed, much better than before her operation. She went first, sniffing the hot air. "Oh, Allie, how often I've thought of this!"

We didn't go as far as the castle, but we did go to the Roman milestone. I told her more about the second Reuben than I had done in my letters, and she said, "I can hardly believe you go to Barleylands and know the old lady. Is she . . . civil to you, Allie?"

"I think she likes me," I said. "She's not a warm person, and I never really know what she's thinking. But I do admire her."

"One never sees the future," Mother murmured. "There at the castle I never imagined I'd have a daughter nearly fourteen, who is free to go to Barleylands."

"I wish you could have done," I said. "I wish the other Reuben hadn't gone away without leaving a message."

"Well, he did," she answered. "But he's been dead a long time and we won't think of him." But I knew as we walked back to the farm for dinner that she *was* thinking of those days, and I showed her the old map when we reached the farm.

Dad had a sleep in the afternoon, and Mother and Mrs. Farmer sat talking in the garden. I sat on the grass near them, listening. I felt strange, not very well, but it was just dread of the parting that was so soon to come. I wished I could know *my* future, all our futures, and be certain that we would be safe in a frightening world.

When they had gone I climbed to the top of one of the haystacks and cried my eyes out. I felt sick and hot, but shivery, too. Adam and Jim had gone rabbiting somewhere and I was glad. I didn't even want my brother on that summer evening. I had fallen in love with so many things and had dreaded going away. Now I wasn't going. Guelder Rose Farm was my home.

After a restive night, when I awoke twice to find that I was crying, I was headachy and quiet at breakfast. But, all the same, there was a certain gladness in my heart that no strange boy or girl would have my view into the apple tree and the use of Mother's books.

I helped Mrs. Farmer to put the finishing touches to the two rooms where the evacuees would sleep. The one on our landing had two beds in it, and the one in the attics also had two beds. The other rooms up there were piled with junk of one kind or another.

"I just hope the children are *clean*," Mrs. Farmer said, as I packed my picnic to take over to the castle.

"They won't be," I remarked, maybe with gloomy relish.

"Well, I've heard tales of poor city children and there are bad slums in Birmingham. But they won't all be poor and dirty, Allie." Mrs. Farmer's warm country voice rose in alarm.

"No, I know. If Adam and I had been evacuated, we wouldn't have been dirty," I agreed. "But they may have fleas and lice, you know."

"Well, it happens in the country, too," she admitted. "The nurse comes regularly to go through the heads in our schools. So you're going off again over the Moss? There's plenty to do here today."

"I'll come back soon as we've had our picnic," I promised, giving Mrs. Farmer a sudden hug. "But I must see Reuben and tell him what's happened. Yes, I know I could have telephoned, but he'll probably have left by now."

It was a cloudy day, but very warm, and I felt rather limp and odd after so much emotion. I walked steadily toward the castle, lost in my thoughts. I was a little late, so Reuben would probably be there already. As I drew near the ruin I glanced up at the tower, but he was not there, nor was he sitting on the stones by the main door. He must be very late, then, for the Moss ahead of me, as I approached, had been pretty well visible all the way to North Guelder. But he'd been late before, when Mrs. Carey delayed him, so I sat down and took out the book I had brought with me. It was John Buchan's *The Thirty-Nine Steps*.

Though I had read it before, it was so exciting and absorbing that I was shocked and startled when I glanced at my new watch. It was twelve o'clock. I sprang up, aware suddenly of how lonely and desolate the place was. I had grown used to being there in the middle of Hunger Moss, but only on that one other occasion had I been quite solitary. Then the sun had been shining, and Reuben had been only twenty minutes late.

Suddenly I was frightened. The ancient castle

loomed above me; the dark hall was behind that gaping, broken doorway. I might have been the only person in the world. But Reuben must be coming across the Moss. And the best way to see was to climb the tower.

It took all my courage to enter the building and to approach the dark stone stairs. But I bridged the gap and began to climb steadily upward. It was a great relief to reach the open roof. The clouds were parting and the sun was breaking through hotly, its light striking a pool here and there. One could see all ways, but at first, sure of success, I looked north. I could see the line of the track clearly all the way to North Guelder and there was no one on it. I turned to look toward the Roman milestone, but he was not there. He was not anywhere in that whole landscape, the second red-haired Reuben.

I stayed on the roof for ten minutes, straining my eyes to watch the far end of the track, a mile away. I could see North Guelder clearly as the sun, breaking quite free of the clouds, struck the golden buildings. I could see Barleylands. I could see the Barleylands herd in a far field, and a red post office van moving along the road that encircled the Moss.

I went slowly and carefully down the steps and back to where I had left my book and my picnic. I sat down, feeling terrible. I was myself and I was Mother . . . waiting there in that lonely place for a boy who never came. It seemed as if life had come full circle.

146

I thought of Reuben on one side of the green gate and me on the other. I had said I would telephone him if I had to go away; *he* couldn't phone me directly, but in a crisis he could have spoken to Mrs. Cox at the post office and she would have brought the message.

Time for me was all mixed up, as if it had happened to me before. It was as if I had always known it would happen again and that I had been subconsciously waiting for it.

The second Reuben had gone away and not sent a message.

11 The Evacuees

I suppose my reaction was so strong because I was already in rather an emotional state. It took me more than fifteen minutes to realize that I *wasn't* in Mother's position. I was perfectly free to go to Barleylands and ask about Reuben. He had probably left a message there, expecting me to go when he didn't turn up.

In the time I'd been there, almost hypnotized, the Moss had changed from a dream into a nightmare. I hated and feared its silence and strangeness. The moment realization hit me, I sprang to my feet and set off at a dangerous speed over the rough path. I only wanted to get away and never see the place again. I only wanted to get to Barleylands.

Panting and sweating, I came to the plank bridge and climbed the stile. I walked through the farmyard and the inner court and found the kitchen door open. Terribly hot, and a bit sick, I burst into the kitchen, to find Emily and the two maids eating their dinner at the huge kitchen table.

"Miss Allie!" Emily cried. She always called me "Miss," which was nearly as nice, and surprising, as "Master." "Where've you been? The mistress thought you'd be over more than an hour ago."

The kitchen was shadowy after the glare of the sun and I was glad, for there were tears in my eyes. "I . . . Mrs. Carey expects me?"

"Yes. You'd better go in. They've nearly finished lunch."

I knew the way to the dining room; a large, grave room that Reuben had shown me. The door was open and Mr. Carey was just rising from the table. When he saw me he said, "Here she is! Well, I'll be off." And he passed me at his usual fast pace, back to work, or at least to supervise work. Mrs. Carey looked across the table, and I stood there in the doorway, feeling shaken still, and very strange.

"Alice, my dear!" she cried. "Don't you feel well? We thought you'd be over a long time ago."

"I . . . I . . ." To my horror I began to cry. She rose in her dignified, leisurely way and approached me. Pulling out a chair, she put me gently into it, saying, "My dear, what's the matter? Reuben told me. . . . Don't cry like that!"

I gasped and sniffed and couldn't find my handkerchief. She handed me a beautifully folded one, smelling of eau de Cologne, and I mopped my nose and face and said shakily, "I'm sorry! Really I am, Mrs. Carey. It's just that such a lot has happened, and then Reuben didn't come to the castle, and it was as if I were Mother all those years ago."

She let me talk, and I told her all about Dad and Mother coming, and how we were to stay at Guelder

150

Rose because there was going to be a war, and how I had waited and waited at the castle and Reuben had never sent a message . . . just like the other Reuben.

"Stop! Stop!" she ordered at last, and I looked up to see her eyes on me, very grave and somehow rather startled. "All this, or most of it, is quite unnecessary, Alice. It's no doubt very upsetting for you that your parents have decided to leave you at Guelder Rose with the Farmers, but it's far the best plan, and I for one am glad to hear it. But to lose yourself in the past . . . I never really understood how much. . . . Don't be absurd, child! Reuben tried to get in touch with you, but Mrs. Cox phoned back to say you'd already left Guelder Rose. Then he said you'd be sure to come straight over the Moss when he didn't arrive at the castle."

"But I couldn't . . . I couldn't! I thought I was Mother." Then I pulled myself together and accepted the glass of water she handed me. "Well, only for a time," I said, when I had drunk deeply. "But it was quite a long time before I realized *I* could come to Barleylands even though she couldn't." I was beginning to be aware that I had completely lost control of myself and my tongue in front of this cool, assured woman I'd admired from the very first moment. She wouldn't admire *me* after such a scene.

Mrs. Carey crossed to a bell and pressed it, and when the younger maid appeared she said, "Katie, I don't believe Miss Alice has had any lunch. Ask Emily for some of that very good soup, and some cold meat and salad." Katie bobbed in an old-fashioned way and went away, and Mrs. Carey turned to me again. "You're fond of Reuben, Alice?"

Fond? In a scared, startled way I had a revelation. I knew that I loved Reuben for all he was, and had been, to me, during the past weeks. His nice sun-tanned face and strong easy body, his voice, and his whole personality, as well as his good mind, had made him the best companion I had ever had, or dreamed of. If it wasn't love then it was a mixture of love and friendship and admiration. I was all but fourteen and he was fifteen, and Mrs. Farmer had said. . . . Then the thoughts had gone, to be remembered later in solitude.

"Of course I am," I said. "We're friends, I hope. At least, we *were* friends. He's gone and perhaps he won't come back for ages."

She laughed. "No, he hasn't gone, Alice. Only for a few hours, anyway. His mother telephoned soon after ten-thirty, just before Reuben was due to leave to meet you. The London telephone lines are jammed because of the growing feeling that war will be declared in a day or two, and she'd been trying to get through for two hours. She asked us to send Reuben to Oxford in the car to catch a London train. She felt he couldn't go after today, as the trains will be full of evacuees tomorrow. They're having lunch at the Paddington Hotel, and his father will get there, too, if he can manage it. Then Reuben will come back on the three o'clock train."

"Oh!" I stared at her blankly.

"It seems possible," said Mrs. Carey quietly, "that Reuben will stay here, just the way you are doing at Guelder Rose. I don't think he'll like the idea much at first, but his father, my grandson, has an even more forceful personality than Reuben himself."

Reuben on the other side of the Moss whatever happened! Oh, I could bear the anxiety and fear so much better if I had his companionship. But . . . "Reuben will want to stay in London," I said. "Only children and young people aren't free, are they? They can't chose. They have no rights."

"That's as it should be," Mrs. Carey answered briskly. "Rights! Who talks like that? Not your parents?"

"Reuben himself," I said, remembering a conversation on the Moss.

"Then he was talking rubbish!" snapped the nearly eighty year old. "London will be bombed, and we have the right to get children away."

"All those evacuees," I murmured, for I found I wasn't scared of her any more. It was a glorious feeling. We eyed each other, woman to woman, rights or no rights. "Ten and a teacher."

"*Touché*, Alice Baker," said old Mrs. Carey. "They'll be here tomorrow and my peaceful life will be over. Well, Reuben will be here to help, and you and that brother of yours can come over and help to organize whenever Mrs. Farmer can spare you. How many is she expecting?"

"Four."

"She won't like it any more than I do, but it's going to happen." The door opened and Katie entered with a tray. She arranged my meal on the unused part of the table; hot soup, homemade bread and butter, meat and salad, and trifle thick with cream.

"I'll leave you to eat," Mrs. Carey said. "Make a good meal."

I sat alone in that big, solemn room and ate as if I had starved for a week. It was only when I had finished that I thought of how I had to walk back across the Moss, and I was horrified to find that I dreaded it. Things had turned out all right, but I knew it would be a long time before I really shook off the awful wait at the castle. I had *lost* the Moss. I couldn't climb the stile and cross the plank bridge. I'd have to walk all the way around the outside.

While I sat there with a dreadful feeling of loss, Mrs. Carey returned. "Alice, I've ordered the car for you. Henderson will drive you back to Guelder Rose. And Reuben will bicycle around to see you before the influx starts tomorrow."

So the Barleylands chauffeur drove me back in fine style, and I didn't have to set foot on the Moss.

By five-thirty in the morning on Friday, September 1, I was awake and kneeling by my window, looking into the apple tree where the fruit was growing ripe. Now that summer was almost over, the sun was rising much later and first light was just beginning to pierce

154

the mist. The air was very warm and quite windless. Out there in the Moss the castle would be growing visible. It was awful to feel a dull misery when I thought of Hunger Moss. The secret, lovely place that had changed so much yesterday. Or maybe the Moss hadn't changed; it was my confusing experience there that had changed my attitude to it.

I turned my thoughts to the children who would be assembling in a few hours' time, ready to start on an adventure that was not of their choice, and I wondered who would sleep at Guelder Rose that night, and how they would feel.

I wondered, jealously, if they would want to go over the Moss, and if they would take possession of the castle. Yes, my thoughts were back there almost at once. I didn't feel as if I would ever want to go there again, but I didn't like the thought of other young people knowing it. Most likely they would be scared; the poor kids would be frightened of everything, homesick and unhappy.

The household had already stirred, and I washed and dressed hurriedly and ran downstairs. I didn't ask Adam to go with me because he always kept out of the way until milking was over, but of late I had sometimes done some of my jobs early. It was no hardship on warm mornings, but I had never been as early as this, and Mr. Farmer, drinking a hurried cup of tea, looked at me in surprise. So did Mrs. Farmer, when she bustled in from the scullery.

"What an early bird! Couldn't you sleep?"

"Not very well," I said. I poured myself a cup of tea and drank it slowly. "I'll let the hens and ducks out and start feeding."

It was still a little misty, and dew beaded the grass as I walked around the hen houses. As the hens were released, they made a warm, contented, clucking sound, and the cock began to crow loudly. When I looked into the pigsties, the pigs started up an eager grunting. "Not your feeding time yet," I said, and went to get hen food.

Oh, an ordinary morning, it seemed, and yet it wasn't ordinary. Mr. and Mrs. Farmer, alert to world news at last, had brought the wireless into the kitchen and we heard the news over breakfast. German troops had invaded Poland, and German planes were raiding Warsaw and other Polish cities.

Nine o'clock brought Miss Jones and Mrs. Baron, the two women who had come originally about the evacuees, and they said the reception center at East Marshland would be opening that morning, with the first children arriving by midday.

"Work must go on, war or no war," Mr. Farmer had said. "We'll get into that field of late wheat. The country'll need food."

So Jim and the men were already up the fields and Adam went to join them. I hung around, doing odd jobs, hoping that Reuben would come. Before he went out

Adam said, "It's a rum do, Allie. They'll all be a lot stranger than we were."

"Only a month," I answered, "and we belong here. You do like it, don't you?"

"Yes, I like it. Only it seems strange, us not in Liverpool with Dad and Mother."

There had been a letter that morning to tell us they had reached home safely. If I didn't think too much about it, I was all right.

Reuben came at ten o'clock. I was in the kitchen garden, picking late runner beans, when I heard his bicycle bell. And there he was outside the green gate, looking just as usual, except perhaps a little more grave.

I was so glad to see him that I forgot all else. He *was* staying and didn't much like the idea. "Feels like funking," he said. "I'd sooner have seen it out in London, but my father said. . . . Well, it wasn't any use arguing, though I tried. I'm to go to school in Oxford, and Great-grandmother says you are, too. Oh, Allie, the one thing that makes it bearable is that you're here as well."

"I feel the same about you," I said. "But what's it going to be *like?* Nothing will ever be the same again, will it?"

"Probably not," Reuben agreed. And yet everything in South Guelder was just the same, peaceful and quiet in the sun.

We cycled over to East Marshland, I on my splendid new bicycle, and found a hive of activity in the village hall, where strangers and some local people were all ready to receive the children. Lemonade and sandwiches were being brought in, and a corner was roped off as an office, with long lists laid out on a table. It seemed, in a way, all part of a dream, for the beautiful village lay in hot sunshine, as yet untouched by little strangers from a big city.

But the strangers began to appear at twelve-thirty, when the first bus drove down the lane. Reuben said, "I'd better be off home. Great-grandmother expects me to be there to soften the blow. I'll be in touch, Allie, or you come over when you can."

As he rode off, the bus drew up. It was crammed with youngish boys and girls. They began to scramble off, and each had a gas mask, luggage of some kind, though not much, and a label fastened to their chests. They were as pale as we had been when we came from Liverpool, and they were shabby and, yes, pretty dirty in some cases. There were two teachers with them, a man and a woman. They didn't look very happy.

I helped to dole out sandwiches and lemonade, but before everyone was supplied another bus arrived, with older boys and girls. These were a much tougher lot, aggressive and inclined to push and fight. Their voices were loud, and the man teacher with them yelled, "You lot, shut up! Get into a line. Billy Mason, any more trouble from you, my lad, and you'll go back to Birmingham."

"Thanks very much, Sir!" retorted a boy of about

eleven with loud derision. "Never wanted to leave it and come to the bloody country."

"And keep your language clean!"

Billy Mason said something much worse and got clipped over the ear. I felt I rather liked Billy; he was like the kids in Liverpool.

The Vicar, Mr. Cressington, was one of the helpers, and he had snatched up a list. "Billy's one of yours at Guelder Rose," he said to me. "With his younger brother, Sam, and his two sisters, Violet and Daffodil."

"Daffodil! What a name!" I gasped, and Billy, over-hearing, cried, "She's Dafty! Never gets called Daffo-dil."

"I'm sure you mean Daffy," I said, feeling curiously glad about Billy, though he'd be a handful. "Well, you're all coming to live with me. Where are your brother and sisters?"

Billy pointed to a rough-looking little boy of eight or nine, and twins who were in between, about ten. Billy and Sam had fair hair, but the girls were reddish. Might have been pretty hair if it had been clean. I thought of poor Mrs. Farmer and nits.

"Don't want to live with anyone, only our mam," Billy said.

"I know, but it's just the same for me. I come from Liverpool, and I've a brother called Adam. You'll like Guelder Rose, really."

"Oh, get lost!" snapped Billy, or less polite words to that effect. "We wanna go home!"

159

"You'd better go home, Alice," Mr. Cressington whispered to me. "They'll be driven over soon. Mrs. Farmer'll need you."

I rode very fast through the sweet-smelling lanes and swooped down into South Guelder. Mr. and Mrs. Farmer and Adam had nearly finished their dinner, and I flung myself breathlessly into my place. "They've come, and it's a whole family. Two boys and twin girls. They'll be arriving soon and I s'pose they'll want something to eat. There were sandwiches and things, but it was all a bit disorganized once they began to pour in."

"The good Lord preserve me!" cried Mrs. Farmer piously.

The Lord didn't preserve her for very long. Within thirty minutes there was the sound of piercing howls outside and, when we rushed to the back door and around the corner of the house, there were the four Masons with one of the women teachers. The teacher was young and pretty and looked nearly in tears herself, but it was Violet and Daffodil who were making all the noise.

"You're too *big* to cry like that!" the teacher was saying. "Don't be silly, Vi and Daffy. It's a lovely place."

"It's a heckuva place!" said Billy. "The country! We all want our mam, and some chips, and where's the pictures?"

They were all brought into the kitchen. The teacher, who was Miss Beryl Raine, was to be billeted at the Vicarage with the other children. She said she must get

160

over there at once and dashed off, and Mrs. Farmer remarked, "She has a headache and small wonder! Now, you four, if you're going to live with me we'd better get to know each other. My husband has gone back up the fields because he has to work hard. I'm Mrs. Farmer, and these are Adam and Alice Baker."

Vi and Daffy cried louder than ever, as if they were five years old and not quite big girls, and Mrs. Farmer said in despair, "We'd better feed them. That's the answer."

But it wasn't. Faced with plates of roast beef, vegetables, and potatoes, the Masons stared blankly and Sam joined in the tears. Mrs. Farmer looked staggered, but Adam and I understood. We knew about the things eaten by poor children in Liverpool.

"Give 'em some bread and jam," said Adam.

At once Vi and Daffy stopped crying and looked alert, and Sam sniffed, wiped his nose on his hand and said, "Jam!"

"That's more like it," Billy said.

Mrs. Farmer, looking truly horrified, removed the good beef and substituted one of her crusty loaves, butter, and homemade raspberry jam. She poured out lemonade. It all disappeared rapidly.

Adam took charge of Billy and Sam and led them upstairs, and Mrs. Farmer and I followed with the girls, leading them up to the attics. Vi and Daffy, clutching their few belongings, burst into tears again when they saw the room prepared for them. It was quite pretty, too, with cretonne curtains and a view over my apple tree.

"What's the matter with them now, Allie?" Mrs. Farmer asked, and I said, "I expect it looks lonely. They probably slept all together at home."

"Well, I never!" she said, shocked.

She had shock after shock during the next few hours and during Saturday. Life was certainly not peaceful with the Masons at Guelder Rose.

On Sunday morning we all sat in the big kitchen and listened to the Prime Minister's speech, telling us that we were at war with Germany. Outside the window the goldenrod moved gently in the warm wind, and I sat staring at it incredulously. At war . . . and it was my fourteenth birthday. I somehow thought I would never like goldenrod again.

12 Others on the Moss

This story is not really about the evacuees, but our Mason family played their part in my tale. I have realized more and more as I wrote that this is about me and the Moss. Hunger Moss—always somewhere in my mind from my earliest years.

From the first moment of our Birmingham family's arrival, I knew I must do my best to help. It started practically enough with my helping Mrs. Farmer to wash all their heads. I ran to buy some medicated soap from Mrs. Cox, and we set to work in the face of violent and noisy protests. Billy's language was awful, and the others' wasn't much better, but the girls were surprisingly pretty after the operation, with shining red-gold hair, and we made them look in a mirror and admired them.

"They ain't pretty!" said Billy, in disgust. But the twins, cheering up, smiled at their own images. We got them all to bed, after several disrupted hours when nothing went right, and in the night I awoke and heard desolate sobbing from up above. So I crept up the attic stairs and talked to Vi and Daffy, and finally they fell asleep in the lavender-scented little beds. Far from home, like me; yet I already felt that Guelder Rose was home in a way.

The biggest shock for us, perhaps, was when Billy and Sam walked unconcernedly almost under the hooves of the cart horses, and laughed at our alarm.

"Our dad works with dray horses," Billy said scornfully. "Us was nearly born in a stable."

They weren't afraid of the cows, either, and somehow soon knew that Adam *was*. It was very trying for Adam.

I didn't see Reuben on Saturday, but after dinner on Sunday I cycled around the Moss to find out how things were at Barleylands. The road gave me occasional glimpses of the Moss, and still I knew I didn't want to go there. I had no idea how I was to explain to Reuben, for I couldn't really tell him the truth; that his absence had created a nightmare. I felt a nagging unhappiness and shame, as well as a sense of loss.

Barleylands was in the same state of chaos as Guelder Rose and the Vicarage. The ten children were all boys, quite big boys of ten and eleven, and they were noisy and aggressively homesick. They didn't know what to do in the country, any more than we had done at first, and the house and garden rang with their shouts. A fight was going on in the courtyard as I arrived. Emily poured out the story of their iniquities.

"It's awful, Miss Allie! Two of them smoking in bed; might have burned the house down. Quite dirty, and scorning good food! That teacher with them, Mr.

Barnes, has no idea of discipline. He spent the whole of yesterday evening in the pub. Master Reuben's been wonderful. They listen to him . . . well, sometimes. The mistress said they must stick to the west wing, but not a bit of it. It's noise and breaking things all the time, and outdoors they fight, and throw things at the animals, and leave gates open."

Oh, dear! Gates! *We* had been no better on that score.

"They're sure to settle down," I said. "And school opens tomorrow. You'll have some peace while they're there, Emily."

Reuben came in then. "You're hearing the tale, Allie? How is it with you? Poor kids, it isn't their fault. They didn't *want* to come."

"How is Mrs. Carey?" I asked.

"Lying down. It's hit her hard. The noise has been ghastly, and a valuable vase got broken. They're not bad kids, really; just tough and independent, and they don't understand anything. I do my best, but they think I'm too posh." And he grinned.

I remembered that Adam had also thought him posh.

"Emily says you can manage them," I remarked.

"Up to a point. I'm better than that rotten teacher, Mr. Barnes. He's a stinker; more interested in his own boredom. Well," added Reuben honestly, "it isn't much fun for him. He's just got engaged, and hates leaving his girl. She's saying she'll join one of the Services. He doesn't like the country any more than the boys do. I know how they all feel."

165

"So do I," I agreed grimly, remembering Adam again. But Adam had changed quite quickly, and maybe some of the evacuees would, too.

Reuben and I climbed secretly to the top of a haystack and lay there in the crackly stuff, quietly talking, although we knew perfectly well we should have been organizing something down below. We talked about the declaration of war, and how strange and frightening it was, and wondered if there would be air raids at once on the cities. It was a heavenly day, so warm and still. Hard to imagine the horrors going on in Poland.

Reuben asked me to stay to tea but I said I'd better go back and help Mrs. Farmer. Our four had spent the afternoon with the Vicarage crowd, but would be back for tea. So Reuben walked through the village with me as I pushed my bicycle. There were two little strangers sitting on the doorstep of the closed post office and store, and Reuben greeted them by name and said to me, "Mrs. Crowe had room for those two, as her daughter got married, and there are two more at Rose Cottage, with one of the women teachers next door. The village children won't play with them yet. Look!" And we saw that the eight village children were sitting under some bushes at the edge of the duck pond. They had a secretive air, as if they were planning mischief, or some move against the evacuees.

"It'll be better when they're all in school," I said hopefully. "They'll soon make friends then."

"And we'll get some peace. Shall we meet at the castle tomorrow?"

At the castle? Oh, why couldn't I slay the dragon of nightmare remembrance of being there alone, meet him, and be happy again? But I would have to go alone on that familiar track. I would see the castle ahead and not be sure he was there. But he *would* be there, and, if he wasn't, I'd know it was just another crisis.

I didn't understand myself, for I knew I wasn't Mother, and the thing had happened, and wouldn't happen again. But I said, "Oh, let's meet on the bikes. I'll leave at eleven and go the East Marshland way around. Let's go to Oxford again. I feel I'd like to see a city. Perhaps it'll be different."

So we went to Oxford and it wasn't really different at all. Life was just going on and there was a lot of traffic. When I returned to Guelder Rose, Adam and the Masons were home from school and Adam looked quite cheerful.

"It was O.K.," he said to me, when we spoke alone. "A bit overcrowded, but we did some interesting work. Miss Jason *expects* you to work, and she said I showed promise and she didn't know why I hadn't won a scholarship."

"Didn't you tell her you were just lazy?" I asked, and he nodded and said, "Something like that, and she wasn't amused. I'll work there, but every spare moment I'll be out in the fields. They're working tonight to get that wheat in." And he rushed off.

"How did you get on?" I asked Billy, and he said, "I'm not stupid. But it's a darn fool little school, with *roses* growing around the door." There was infinite scorn in his voice.

"Better than a dirty old city playground," I remarked, and he jeered and spat in the dust.

"Something going on *there*. This place is dead from the neck up."

The Masons weren't reconciled to country life, but even in a few days they looked different. The twins had freckled noses and sun-tanned arms and had fallen in love with the new kittens in the barn. They were starting to eat proper meals, too. Mrs. Farmer was more cheerful and said they weren't bad kids, if their language wasn't so terrible. She tackled the problem by buying ice cream and then denying it to any offender. Not altogether fair, maybe, but it began to work. They adored ice cream.

I wasn't happy and would have been glad if it was time to start at my new school. The Moss brooded in my dreams, as it had done during the first days. I knew I had to go back there, but still avoided the issue, and somehow I kept Reuben from guessing how I felt. We met on our bicycles all during that week.

After a couple of cloudy, damp days the weather was hotter than ever, with threatening thunder, but a storm didn't break. On the Wednesday, after tea, I took a message to the Vicarage and, coming back, I saw all four Masons just disappearing down the lane that led to the Moss. I felt hot and cross and somehow "all wrong" with myself, and an unreasonable fury surged up in me. I flew after them and caught up with them before they reached the stile.

"You don't want to go near the Moss!" I said loudly, and they all turned around. "It's a dangerous place. You might fall into the bog. I did myself when I first came and I might have been lost forever. Besides, it's *haunted.*"

"Haunted?" They stared at me with wide eyes. Even Billy looked impressed. "What with?"

"Mostly Romans. Most of the ghosts are people who were here a long time ago. That's what the local people believe, anyway."

"Lot of rot!" said Billy, but even he glanced over his shoulder.

"You ask Jim. *He* won't go." Oh, I was so hot, and my head ached, and I couldn't stop myself.

"Don't let's go!" cried Daffy, and they all turned and walked back with me, though Billy had more spirit than the rest and averred loudly that *he* wasn't afraid of ghosts. Anyway, I'd stopped them for the time being, and the castle and the secret place were safe. But I wasn't proud of myself. I'd been feeling so grown up and sensible until that affair at the castle . . . and they might like the Moss and in time learn about flowers and birds, as I had done.

Oh, nothing would be right until I had the Moss back. I was just a silly coward, and mean as well.

Adam was somewhat ruffled in his disposition, too, because it was so very galling for him that the Masons weren't scared of the large animals. Billy and Vi even had a go at milking and did quite well.

I didn't see Reuben on Thursday, but on Friday he arrived at Guelder Rose about ten. "Allie, there's a plan for tomorrow, and Great-grandfather says you can bring your lot over, too. Henderson's really going to organize it, with Mr. Barnes. They've got quite friendly. We're going to have sports in the ten-acre pasture near the house for the evacuees and the village children, but not until evening, because it's too hot to do much in the afternoon. Then a spanking picnic supper, and you, Adam, and the Masons can cram into the car and be driven home when it gets dark."

All kinds of thoughts went through my head, but the main one was that he was taking it for granted that Adam and I would walk the others across the Moss to Barleylands. And I had talked all that nonsense to them about the Moss being haunted! But, if the Masons would go, it might be a way out for me. I'd *have* to go and get it over.

"But will they join in races and things?" I asked. "They don't like being organized. Billy'll tell us to get something worse than lost."

"No, he won't, when you explain there'll be prizes for everything. And that's our job now. We're going to every village shop within miles to buy up all the things

170

they like. Balls, puzzles, and sticky sweets, and mouth organs and trumpets . . . "

"I'll have no trumpets in my house!" Mrs. Farmer interrupted, coming within earshot as we stood in the garden.

"And there'll be hot sausages on sticks, and oceans of ice cream. Let's get going. Great-grandfather's given me a lot of money."

So we rode off to raid village stores, and soon my bicycle basket and a bag Reuben had brought were piled up with prizes. And all the time, as we rode from village to village, I was thinking of the Moss and the Masons, and how I had to make everything come right. Maybe the only way for me to keep the Moss now was to share it.

On Saturday morning I found the Masons all together in the barn, looking at the kittens. Billy and Sam's ideas were more in the nature of teasing and torture, but Vi and Daffy were fiercely protective. They'd have scratched their brothers' eyes out if any harm had come to the small family.

I said, "Look here, you lot! There's sort of a party tonight over in North Guelder. We're going to have an early tea; then we'll walk over. There are lovely prizes for races, and sausages on sticks and ice cream for supper. Then we'll all be driven home in a big car by a chauffeur."

171

"Go on!" said Billy unbelievingly. "Shuvvers are for rich people, like the Lord Mayor of Birmingham."

"Other people have them, too. So you'll come?"

Billy was pretty quick and he'd somehow grasped the layout of the despised countryside. "North Guelder? That's the village t'other side of that Moss place? You said across. But you told us it was haunted. You said . . . "

We were all standing in burning hot, curiously heavy sunshine just within the doorway of the barn. There wasn't a breath of air and I felt sweat trickling down my nose. It was the moment of truth.

"Yes, we'll go across the Moss. It's the quickest way and you'll be safe with me and Adam. It's true that the local people don't like the Moss, but it *isn't* haunted. Not as far as I know." Only haunted by visions of Mother and myself. "It's safe enough when you know the way, now the weather's been good for so long. I said all that because I didn't want you to go. I . . . I thought it was *my* place. I'll tell you why another time."

They looked at me gravely. "Isn't Adam scared?" Sam asked.

"No, he isn't."

"But he doesn't like the cows."

Oh, poor Adam and that wretched herd!

Adam wasn't very keen on the idea of the sports party but he agreed to come. He wasn't quite immune to the promise of good prizes and hot sausages on sticks. But the day was so enervating that I wondered if anyone would have energy for racing. After dinner it was hotter than ever, with a brassy glare.

"It'll thunder," said Mr. Farmer, entering the kitchen as we young ones ate a very early tea. "Best not go."

But thunder had been threatening for days and nothing had happened, and we were expected at Barleylands. I *couldn't* put it off. We had to go across the Moss.

By a quarter to five we were ready to leave, and suddenly there was no sunlight at all, just strange, golden-gray light. Mrs. Farmer looked much disturbed. "Say you get caught halfway over? They'll hold no party tonight at Barleylands. It'll pour."

"Oh, it'll probably pass over," Adam said impatiently.

We set off down the lane and we all climbed the stile. I went first, with Adam following. Once we were on our way I felt better; there was no turning back. The Moss received us with a silence that was even more brooding than usual in the strange light, and the children behind us were very quiet, probably awed.

"Bet it *is* haunted!" said Sam, after quite a long time.

"Well, *I'm* not scared!" said Billy.

We neared the Roman milestone, where the track grew wider. I stopped on the piece of causeway that remained and looked all around; at the castle, grim and dark; at the patches of dully gleaming water. And suddenly I loved the Moss again and my reluctance had quite gone. Yes, even in that awful light, with the hot, still air and no sound anywhere, not of a single bird.

Haunted it might well be, but it was mine, and could be the Masons if they wanted it.

Another day I'd show them the secret place and how to climb the tower. When winter came we none of us could go there, but there was time yet, and the Moss was big enough, and strange enough, to accept other children.

13 A Simple Explanation

The "other children" huddled close together and Adam said, "Oh, get on, Allie! What are you dreaming for? It's getting dark!"

And so it was, at not much after five. I set off rapidly for Barleylands.

The sky grew blacker and blacker, but there was a golden rim of light almost all the way around the Moss, like gilding on the edge of a saucer. The track was much better beyond the Roman milestone, and I could almost have walked it blindfolded by that time. Instinct told me where the bad places still were and I skirted them, shouting warnings. But if it poured with rain before we reached the plank bridge, there might well be trouble. We should have listened to the Farmers. I had meant to share the Moss with the Masons, not terrify them. But, in spite of Vi and Daffy's tears on the first day, they were tough enough children. Daffy did say, "I don't like it!" but Billy retorted roughly, "You shurrup, our Dafty! We're nearly there."

He was right. Dim, yet vaguely gold touched, we could see North Guelder village, and the church and the big group of buildings that was Barleylands. There was the plank bridge and the stile. I had brought them safely across the Moss and I was filled with relief on that score, and with joy because the Moss was mine again and I had seen it in its strangest mood.

"There's going to be the father and mother of a storm!" Adam said in my ear, as he climbed the stile close behind me. "We'll only just make it."

I turned toward the lane that led to the farmyard gate without thinking at all. I never entered Barleylands by the front gate unless I cycled, and not always then. The natural way was to the kitchen or side doors. As we almost ran over the hard-baked ruts, a vivid flash of lightning ripped the sky wide open. It was fork lightning such as I had never seen before.

The twins screamed and Sam gave a kind of yelp. I had a strong instinct to fling myself on my face, for there were trees overhead here and there, and trees got struck by lightning. But I kept on and reached the farmyard gate, which was open. A violent clap of thunder had come close on top of the lightning, but in the intense silence that followed I heard a steady throbbing from the great cowshed. That was the sound of the milking machine, so milking wasn't over.

And then Reuben was there, running between the barns from the inner courtyard. "Gosh! You're here!" he shouted. "I thought maybe you wouldn't come. Great-grandmother said Mrs. Farmer would stop you. We aren't going to have any sports at this rate."

"She tried," I said shakily. "But Adam and I thought . . . it's been thundery for days. Where are the others?"

"Our kids are in the harness room with Henderson and Mr. Barnes. The village children haven't come yet. We were waiting for you all, and then it suddenly grew so dark. Oh, I say!" And Reuben ducked as another fork seemed literally to pass overhead. The thunder crashed with it, and we all watched, hypnotized, as the fork of lightning ripped along the roof of the barn nearest the cowshed. It was a very old roof, covered with dry moss, and underneath the golden tiles were, as I very well knew, thick and ancient wooden beams. Almost quicker than it takes to tell, flames sprang up and the top of the building began to burn.

A good many things happened at once. Mr. Carey and two of the men appeared in the cowshed doorway (lit by a following flare of lightning); Reuben shouted, "I'll telephone the fire brigade!" and rushed away; and the twins and Sam flung themselves into a corner and cowered there. Mr. Carey glanced up at the blazing roof, shouted something, and disappeared again, and Billy shrieked, "The cows are in there! Get 'em out!"

Thunder crashed again, but there was no rain at all. The barn was burning fiercely in a minute or two, and when the thunder died away the imprisoned cows, aware of danger, were making a terrible noise.

The Barleylands pedigreed herd numbered some forty cows, each one very valuable. And they were all tethered in their stalls. It would take more than three men to release them quickly. Billy never hesitated. Adam hesitated for a moment, then said, "Oh, heck!"

and followed him into the cowshed. I wondered if I should go, too, but Sam and the twins must be taken to a safer place. There would be a stampede of frightened animals.

I rushed to the children, grabbed as many arms as I could, and pushed them before me between the blazing barn and the one that was safe so far and out into the courtyard, toward the kitchen door of the house. The Barleylands evacuees and Mr. Barnes and Henderson had all come out of the harness room, and Henderson was running out a hose. I pushed the children toward Emily and the maids and ran back to help.

I'd probably done the right thing, but I felt guilty. Adam! Adam, so scared of cows! He'd be trampled, he'd die of terror, I was thinking. When I looked through the passageway, the herd, lit by a red glare, was surging through the farmyard and into the lane. Going to safety in their pasture, for that gate had been opened.

The passageway was scary, with flames overhead, but I dashed through and saw Mr. Carey, the men, and Adam and Billy in the doorway of the cowshed. One of the men ran across the yard and began to unwind another hose, fastening it to a tap in the wall.

"Reuben's phoned the fire brigade!" I shouted, but I knew the nearest brigade was in Oxford and the whole place would go up before help came. The thin jets of water that started to play on the flames could not combat the growing inferno.

And then I felt a big drop of rain on my sweating face,

178

and another and another. Within a few seconds the downpour had started, and it would save Barleylands. Smoke and steam made the air unbreathable, and I was getting soaking wet. I dived into a little byre, where calves were kept in bad weather, and Billy and Adam rushed to join me. "What a do!" Adam gasped.

"Those cows might have made roast meat!" said Billy. "Where are our kids, Allie?"

"I took them to the house. You were both very brave," I said, feeling very shaky and with my throat so dry I almost choked.

"Billy untied more than I did," Adam told me. I knew it was no time, in front of young Billy, to say that probably he'd never be scared of cows again, having saved the Barleylands herd, so I said nothing but just gazed out, watching as the rain began to beat the flames.

By the time the firemen came it was nearly out, and all they had to do was to tear down beams that were still smouldering and try to make the area safe from a damaged wall.

We had to go around the buildings to the house, and when we got there we were very wet. The evacuees were all in the kitchen with Emily and the maids, who were soothing them with some of the ice cream meant for supper. We were glad to eat ice cream, too, to soothe our throats. Emily was very much upset, but Mr. Carey looked in to say that all was well and to thank Billy and Adam for their prompt action. Reuben, who had been acting as go-between, went off to tell his great-grandmother, and Emily said to me, "Miss Allie, you're soaking wet, and the boys aren't much better. I must find some dry clothes. The boys are easy, but you, Miss Allie . . ."

She led me to a large bedroom and offered me towels to rub myself down; then she produced a pink silk dressing gown belonging to Mrs. Carey. As Mrs. Carey and I were much of a height it fitted well, but I felt it was somehow wrong to wear her beautiful robe.

"Your own things'll be dry soon as I can manage," said Emily, returning as I tied the sash around my waist. "And now the mistress wants to see you."

"*Now?*" I asked, for I felt shaky and, in spite of the wetting, I was still terribly hot. The storm and rain hadn't cooled the air.

"In the drawing room," she said. "Go on, Miss Allie, talk to her. She's had a bad few days, and this, coming on top . . ."

So I went slowly downstairs, feeling quite unlike myself, and Emily knocked at the door and announced, "Miss Allie." Mrs. Carey was sitting in a deep chair near the ornate, empty fireplace and my first thought was that she looked old. I had never really thought that before. The storm was passing over but the light was still dim and I could only just see her. The impression was of someone of great age. Yet her voice was quite brisk.

"Sit down, Alice," she said. "I'm sorry you all had

such a frightening experience. And Reuben says Adam was very brave."

"Well, he was," I said. "Adam's big trouble has been his fear of cows. So he was braver than Billy, even if he is older."

"He's a good boy. My husband met Bert Farmer the other day and he's very pleased with Adam. Oh, come in, Katie! Put the tray here and switch on that little lamp." The smell of good coffee rose up from the tray, and Katie began to pour out. "I hope it's strong," said Mrs. Carey. "We both need it."

I did need it and I soon began to feel better, though I wished I were dressed and not naked under Mrs. Carey's pink robe, with damp hair tickling my hot neck. Mrs. Carey drank two cups of coffee, then said, "Many things seem to have been happening lately, not all of them pleasant. I had meant to speak to you before this, Alice. Go over to that desk in the corner and switch on the lamp near it. The key is in the lock of the desk. Turn it."

Astonished, wondering, I obeyed, and the front of the desk opened. It seemed a very old piece of furniture, with many drawers. There was a lot of carving.

"Pull out the bottom drawer on the left." I did so, and it came out easily in my hand. "There's another drawer behind . . . a secret drawer. These old desks so often have them. There's a little knob at the side; press it. Now pull out the second drawer."

181

Clumsily, awkwardly, I tried to obey and found the secret drawer. Inside was an envelope. "Bring it to me," said Mrs. Carey.

I picked up the envelope and couldn't help seeing the large, clear, youthful writing. "Miss Mary Selby, Guelder Rose Farm, South Guelder, Oxfordshire." My hand was shaking as I handed it to her. Nothing seemed real in that large, beautiful room, with the storm dying away outside.

Mrs. Carey looked at me steadily. "Alice, I'm a proud woman, but not quite as proud as I used to be. I was obstinate, and firm in my opinions and very loyal to my husband. But over this matter I always knew that I was wrong. That fact is proved by the way I kept this letter, though I hadn't thought of it for years until you came and I heard how you felt about your mother's experiences on the Moss. You identified with her that day Reuben didn't meet you, and I knew then I'd have to pocket my pride and confess my fault. The affair wasn't dead . . . you made that very clear. So here is the letter that the other Reuben asked me to send to Mary Selby. He would have posted it himself, but he hadn't a stamp and he went away in a considerable hurry. His parents wouldn't wait."

"Oh, Mrs. Carey!" I whispered. So simple an explanation. There *had* been a message and it had never been sent, because of . . .

"I never liked that friendship," Mrs. Carey said. "For one thing I disliked Reuben spending so much time on the Moss, and for another, as I gather you know, there was extremely bad feeling between my husband and the Farmers at that time. I was displeased with Reuben for making a friend of a girl from Guelder Rose, though I knew nothing at all about Mary Selby. She never came here. You certainly know that, too."

I was shocked, and yet suddenly happy. It seemed awful that Mrs. Carey was having to say such things to me, yet, oh, it was wonderful to know that the other Reuben had cared enough to write that letter.

"Send it to your mother, Alice, if you think she still wants it now. Apologies seem hardly suitable. I see I did her a great wrong, when she was very young and vulnerable. Though," and she sighed, "we are all vulnerable all the time, and age makes no difference."

"I *will* send it," I said, for the letter would lay a kind of ghost. "Mother has Dad and us, but those days waiting at the castle did something to her. I understand." And I shivered slightly, though I was so hot, as I remembered my own quite short waiting,

"Well, that's that," she said briskly. "I'm faulty, like most human beings. Perhaps you'll show kindness to me by not mentioning it to anyone else, even your brother."

"I won't tell anyone," I said, and rose and hesitated. I would have been glad, somehow, to kiss that calm, controlled face, but she didn't invite it. "Thank you, Mrs. Carey. I see why you did it."

"Do you?" she asked grimly. "It was a mean, petty

thing to do to two children. Well, no doubt you'll all have your sports and supper next week. As soon as your clothes are dry Henderson will drive you all home. By the way, I telephoned to Mrs. Cox to ask her to let Mrs. Farmer know you're all safe. It was a silly thing to do to cross the Moss with a storm brewing."

Holding the letter in my hand I went slowly out of the room. Emily pounced on me as I stood in the hall. "Come into the little library, Miss Allie. I have your clothes drying in front of the kitchen fire, and they won't be long. How is the mistress?"

"I don't know," I answered. "She looks . . . older, Emily."

"We all are after this week," Emily retorted and left me alone in a room full of books. I sat down in a leather chair and sat staring at the other Reuben's letter.

184

14 No Entry

Two years have passed. It is September, 1941, and Adam and I are still in South Guelder, though not at Guelder Rose.

The Masons went home at Christmas, 1939, because nothing much was happening (it was called the phony war), and most of the other evacuees went with them. I think that, by then, Billy was sorry to go, but their parents wanted them back.

It wasn't until spring, 1940, that the war really hotted up, and eventually other evacuees came. We never heard what happened to the Masons when Birmingham was bombed. I hope they were all right. I liked them all and they did play their part in my story.

Reuben and I go to school in Oxford and our friendship has deepened. We usually cycle together in fine weather, though we have to take different buses in dark of winter. Adam did well at East Marshland school. He's fourteen now and has just won a scholarship to a school in Oxford. He still says he wants to go in for farming, but he won't be an ordinary farm laborer. Maybe he'll go to an agricultural college, if he works hard enough.

Reuben will be eighteen before Christmas and he may be going to Balliol College, Oxford, next year, but that will all depend on the war. If only he can go there he won't be far away, though of course he could grow so grand as an Undergraduate that he won't bother with me any more.

When the English cities began to be bombed it was terrible to be isolated in South Guelder, and I can't even write of my feelings when the nightmare bombings of Liverpool came in spring, 1941. The shop was destroyed and our house in Green Street badly damaged by blast, and, when it was all over, Dad and Mother, who had escaped by being in an air raid shelter, came to Guelder Rose. Mrs. Cox had retired and someone else had taken over the store and post office, but she didn't like it and eventually Dad and Mother took over the business and Adam and I moved out of Guelder Rose with them. Now I have a tiny bedroom overlooking the village street.

I know Mother loves running the post-office side of the business, and I believe she's deeply happy to be living in South Guelder. I'm not quite so sure of Dad, though he joins in community things and seems to be accepted. He belongs to the local Home Guard and takes his turn at watching at night for invaders. Maybe Dad will always be a town person, but I am so glad we're all together in a safe place.

The Moss. . . .Yes, I've seen it lying under snow. For two springs I saw the wild iris and the marsh marigolds and many rarer plants. I love it more than I ever did, and I think I've lost it forever.

For yesterday an Army truck drove up and parked near the top of the lane, and men got out and began to erect a huge board. The board said: WAR DEPARTMENT. NO ENTRY. VERY STRICTLY PRIVATE. And, when I cycled around the Moss to North Guelder this morning, there was the same kind of board at the stile by the plank bridge, and rumor has it that the whole Moss is going to be an Army training ground; maybe, one day, a bombing range.

There are even rumors that the villages will be evacuated, but Mr. Carey says it isn't true. He has a close friend who works at the War Office. Mr. Carey has put a manager over the farm and doesn't work so hard. Mrs. Carey is still alive, but the war has taken its toll of her; and increasing age, too, I suppose.

When I spoke to her alone today she said, "If it isn't over by next year Reuben will want to join up, and leave Balliol until later. Has he said anything to you, Alice?"

"No," I answered, but I felt sick. He hadn't *said* he wanted to join up when he was old enough, but he did talk an awful lot about the RAF. In any case he hadn't a hope of staying out of the war for long; maybe she hadn't realized that he would be called up if he didn't volunteer.

I was sixteen last week. If it goes on *I* can join one of the Services and go far away from South Guelder. But I don't think I want to go. I love the villages so, but how will it be without the Moss? Shut away from it, forbidden to go down the lane and climb the stile. My own beloved place, so near and lost to me. They are building an Army camp in a field by the crossroads, where South Guelder Hall used to stand. The Hunger Arms will be full of soldiers, and South Guelder will have to accept them, as it accepted the evacuees. And will they tell the strangers that the Moss is haunted? I hope they do.

I'm going to the top of the church tower to look over the Moss. Mr. Cressington hasn't retired; he says he'll stick to his post while things are bad. The tower is the lookout post for the Home Guard and is kept locked against outsiders now. But I have a key to the ancient door.

So I'll always be able to see the Moss, though the Vicar says I'll get shot as a spy if anyone sees me up there. He wasn't entirely joking, either. I know they'll spoil it and take away its secrets; they'll make another road . . . well, the Romans made one. Things do have to change, but I think I've lost forever my dream of Hunger Moss, and soon I'll be grown up.

ABOUT THE AUTHOR

MABEL ESTHER ALLAN decided she was going to be a writer when she was eight and sold her first short story at nineteen. Many years later she sold a book, the first of over one hundred she has written for young people. Except for the war years when she served in the Women's Land Army and did some teaching, Miss Allan has been a full-time author. She lives now in Heswall, Merseyside, England, where she works in a room overlooking the hills of Wales.

Miss Allan is fond of traveling and often draws the backgrounds for her books from places she has visited. Her interests also include the theatre, ballet, photography, and, very specially, folk customs and folk music.